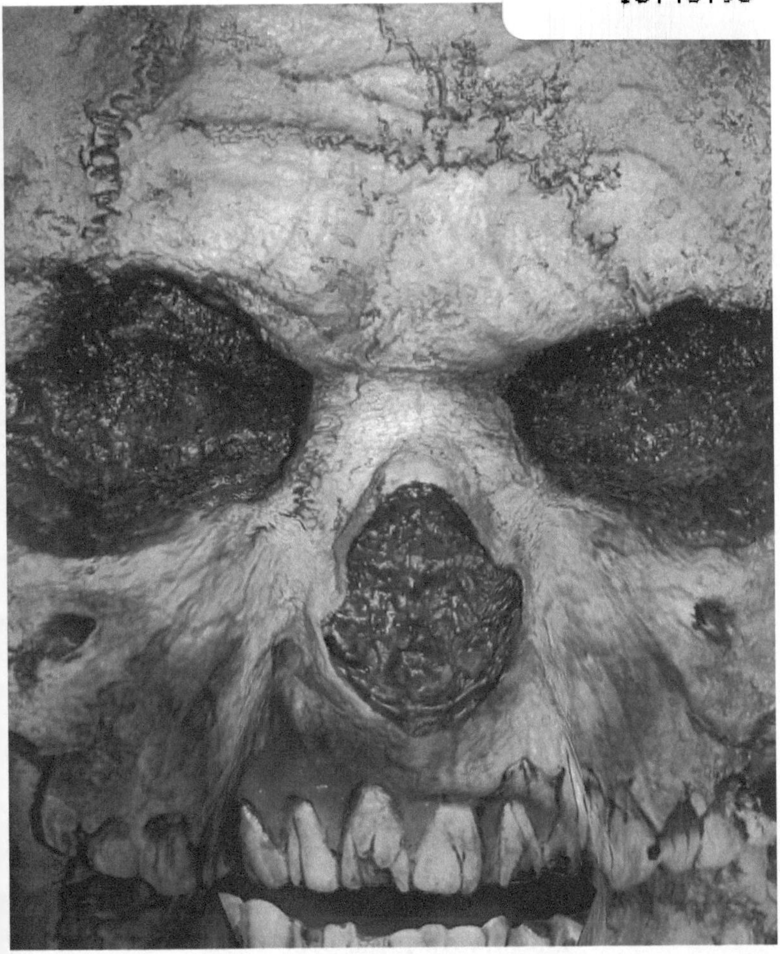

I0745798

The Cruising Deads

**Volume 1 and 1a - Manx Zombies
and The Chosen One
By Divad Thims**

**Manx Zombies First Print Edition 28/11/17
ISBN 13: 978-1912039722
Chosen One First Print Edition (17/1/17)
ISBN 13: 978-1912039005**

**This book contains Volume 1 and 1a of the series.
Volume 1 includes crosswords for each of the Log's,
you can win cool prizes.**

Acknowledgements
To my family and friends, I love you all.

Book design and crosswords by 3ZombieDogs
Published by ThreeZombieDogs
Nobie Publishing, Amsterdam
Photography by: Cameron Smith and Ivan Bliznetsov
Contributing written Submission: Calista Smith
Illustration by Lee Smith
Martin Harley, 'Blues at My Window'

Book Trailer by C J McDaniel & 3ZombieDogs
Film Trailer: Editing and Acting by Voice-over Pete, Allie Madison,
Sebski, script by Divad Thims

New Zealand (Rainbow Warrior Memorial) via Wikimedia Commons.
Stock images by Pixabay. Printed by (a) Ingram, Amazon and other
distributors may have rights to print with publishers permission. (b) Book
Printing UK, Woodston, Peterborough. All printing should adhere to
recycle and sustainable policies. Distribution by Ingram, Amazon &
3ZombieDogs. Fonts by Bradley Hand ITC, Woodcutters. Logo by Designs
Corner and Kingprabath

Citations: The word 'Earthlings' was used as a title in a documentary film by director Shaun Monson called "Earthlings." The word 'Earthanity' is a title to a book by author Southwater. The term 'Toxicity in the gut' was also used in the book 'The Forbidden Ones' by Zed x Syndra. And the term '1984,' from one of my best loved books '1984' by George Orwell.

Dedicated to World Leaders

When Donald Trump won the American election, I watched an interview on UK TV; one pompous ass stated: "…its not what I fear Trump will do to us Americans! It's what I am afraid he will NOT do for the UK and Europe. Who will protect your countries now?"

To that pompous ass, I say: Who will protect you from the DeadS? Silly question, of course 'The Chosen One" will, or at the very least she will try!

Lets hope the world leaders, lead their country to live in harmony with each other throughout the world and in harmony with our planet. And accept the freedom of rights of others. Borders are one of the destructing forces to the earthling race.

**No DeadS were harmed in writing this
first book in the series of:**

Volume 1: The Chosen One

Volume 1 should be read first before reading any others. The story is carried forward in Volume 2. Volume 1a and 1b are equally important to the series, and their events occur simultaneously to Volume 1.

Volume 1A: Manx Zombies

You can read Volume 1A at any time before Volume 2. It's a parallel story to Volume 1 occurring on the Nomadic Island of the Isle of Man. The story line will play a paramount role in following the series and its outcome.

Volume 1B: Amsterdam Vampires

You can read Volume 1B at any time before Volume 2 It's a parallel story to Volume 1 occurring in Amsterdam. The story starts to outline Vampires and Vamptures. The story will play a paramount role in following the series and its outcome.

Volume 2: Derry Zombies, Bridge of DeadS

Volume 2's story follows directly on from where volume 1 finished. You should read all previous volumes first.

Other volumes coming soon.

The story as told by 'A Chosen One.' She is given the task by the Divine Gods to find a cure and heal the cracks in the celestial realms. Keeping Logs while travelling from Hollywood to the harbours of New York. She needs to convince every earthling on her travels to go to the cruise ships. The vessels are destined for the safe shores of Derry, Europe, and China. These countries are rich in tradition and hold the answers and the prayers to save Earthanity. The story begins in the year 1000, and the ships set sail to Ireland during 2016. This is Volume 1 of the series of The Cruising DeadS.

We are sure of two things in life, "Birth and Death" what came first? "Earthlings or the DeadS?" The Cruising DeadS is not just another horror Zombie series of stories, or is it? You the reader can be judge and jury!

Origination of the Story. The story started as a prank. Martina loves 'The Walking Dead' and other Zombie/horror films. She wanted to feature as a Zombie. So, I came up with a plot to write a Zombie story and get her involved without her knowing it was me. The idea was to surprise her on her birthday. But the surprise failed when a letter to 'The Cruising DeadS' arrived at our doorstep. However, the story began to evolve as I wrote. I became engrossed and it sprung into a road map towards a series. The story is a series of volumes and I'm loving writing every word. I owe her a great gratitude for getting me to write, but also believing in me and encouraging my writing. Thanks, Darling xx

The Term DeadS

DeadS This is an earthling like creature (Perhaps known as a Zombie, but Not a Zombie) They originates from an other realm in our universe and turns earthlings into what some refer to as the undead or zombie. Their purpose will become clearer as the other volumes are released.

The word is both plural and singular and will not change throughout the book. When the sex of the DeadS is not mentioned, you can use your imagination to their gender.

Vampture This is a creature evolved from the realms of the Vampires. It is a hybrid from a Vampire and Vulture.

A Female Vampture is called Vamture

Vamptures will feature mostly in Volume 1B and from Volume 2 onward in the series of The Cruising DeadS.

Manx Log 1 Nightmares Continue to Haunt

Lumpy Blood dripped frivolously down my devilish cheeks before it landed and splattered on the ships outside wooden deck. Vivid dreaming within my nightmares yet again, awakened by "I am ever so sorry mam" as the young lad bumped me back into reality on the rolling deck. He was making his way to hang over the side and fill the sea with his guts.

Pointing as I shouted, "Look out," but it was too late, the wind succeeded in covering others, with colourful vomit, while they were leaning over the side of the deck waving their last farewells to Liverpool.

He turned towards me with an incandescent smile and proclaimed in the weirdest chat up line I have ever heard, "They are planning to build a new cemetery at Douglas Head", I turned towards him and replied "WHAT?", "People are dying to get in". I managed a smile, as this was my type of humour, something my

Dad would have said to me. I looked straight into his eyes, his knees buckled and trembling as he looked back for a positive response. How could I let him down gently without destroying his young endeavours of courtship in a world already difficult for whom to trust? "Sorry, I' am not into blokes." I stroked his hair and was careful not to touch his puke as I carefully navigated past him.

As I walked away, I filled my lungs with a fulfilling breath of fresh sea air, the smell of disinfectant overcame the natural smells and wonders of our earth.

"These Youngsters, just can't hold their drink" she proclaimed in annoyance, as the deck received another good scrubbing from this old timer. It was to be the final sailing, and "by god it was going to arrive clean and tidy", she murmured under her smoky breath, coughing and spluttering as she mopped, with a 'Rollie' stuck to her upper lip.

While retiring inside for a bite to eat, those hungry pesky seagulls flew over every move I made, in the most annoying manner. "They taste great with spuds and neaps," said the young lad, determined to impress me with his final chat up attempt. He turned away and spewed his guts out yet again over the side of the ship, some fell and splashed across the deck before he had the chance to get his head over the side. At last, the seagulls had their own feed and left me alone to clamber down the stairs to the cafe deck in peace.

Returning to my Manx birth home after only a week away, boy it felt like a year! I recalled many stories of how the locals would form a circle of gossip and tales. This ritual is as strong today as it was when I was born. One story that always brought a smile to my face was the fable lady story. She purchased an apple from the local grocery store and when later that morning she sat down in the cafe for her daily ritual of milky coffee and thick buttered toast she was questioned, "I heard you bought a fruit basket?"

This story outlines the need for the gossipers to fill in the missing blanks and make more of something which indeed, it is not. This ritual has protected the locals and provided optimistic hope of truth and tales including relief from the American troubles.

I relapsed yet again into an open eye dream from my past life.

- I came across a young Wolf, it beckoned me to come closer. Being inquisitive I ventured near, as I did so, it leapt into the air, in a sudden moment of fear, I fell back into a deep ditch filled with murky water. As I struggled for breath, I felt the hand of a small luminous creature pull me from my watery grave.

Starring into its eyes I could sense from its exquisite and colourful eyes that it meant me no harm. It whispered into my ear, "you are a chosen one and you always say good morning to us, we shall meet again to defend both our realms." –

It disappeared as fast as it spoke those words. I did not understand the meaning of this event, until the Deads, Zombies took control of America.

Every encounter, every meeting, even by chance can hold a hidden or special message. It is imperative if you sense this to ask the other person a question, or you could end up taking a pathway that could derail you from your true destiny of your existence.

Manx Log 2 Lady of Mann

The Lady of Mann known as the Lady was a ship well used to a continual recall for assistance to the Manx Fleet and people. Lady was brought back into service when the first attacks struck America and the British forcibly acquired all other seaworthy vessels from the Manx. This was to be the last sailing of the Lady under Manx control as the Brits were now acquiring all ships, to try warp the invasion of the Deads.

The lady set sail from Liverpool for her last journey, bound for Douglas harbour. The seas were choppy and beginning to swell to a degree that would make passengers uncomfortable beyond their belief. Despite the occurrences in America, the Manx people were optimistic and they continued to travel, trade and holiday within Scotland, Wales and England, keeping close to the Isle of Man was still their main priority.

Understandably, everyone was now concerned and wanted to return to their homeland as news of the Cruising Deads arrival in the port of Derry in Ireland. That was just a tad too close for comfort.

In the ships eating deck, the coffee grinder rattled louder than normal in the cafe, drowning out the vivid conversations of the chatty passengers. The main topic of everyone's thoughts and conversations were the new troubles in Ireland and their defiance that the Zombies would definitely not reach Manx Shores.

The Manx were a proud bunch, understandably thinking that the island would be secure and protected from the advancement of the Zombies like it was in the Nomadic Invasion of the Norse. The Manx refused to call them with their true name of 'The Deads', instead, they called them with the old folklore name of "Zombies". The Manx were a superstitious lot, and I was proud to be one of them. My dad did not have that privilege, he was always referred to as a come-over.

I am one of the chosen ones and the Divine Gods have sent me to the nomadic shores of the Manx Island to await the arrival of Petre and to assist in the Manx transition to the new world. The Manx people are not fully aware of the developments within Europe, especially what is currently occurring in Ireland.

The ship contained passengers from every walk of life, it was a diverse passenger list.

- Poor to the rich, business folks to returning holidaymakers –

People intent on making an attempt at a normal life, despite the current American and Irish Deads attacks.

As I looked at the deck I could see the fear on their faces grow as the ship began to rock from side to side. As the Lady of Mann violently rocked in the increasing swell, old wooden tables and chairs that were not fixed to the floor began to cascade across the dining area. Water poured down from the top deck and children screamed as their parents tried frantically to grasp them as they slid across the watery deck.

Manx Log 3 The Ships Turning

A young mother to be cried out in pain! With a sense of impending loss, you could see the fear written on her motherly face. She boarded the vessel against medical advice to be with her family. Her husband was one of the unfortunates butchered by the mindless European military.

Like many others that set sail that day, everyone bound by a common purpose, to survive the sailing and the Zombies.

The Manx shores would provide that safety for her baby, or so she thought.

This was to be a new beginning for the Manx baby, no one could assist her as she began an uncontrollable and painfully birth,

- Earthlings were gripping solid objects to save

themselves –

even I was powerless to help. I did try to help, many times, but the ferocity of the storm and the ships violent manoeuvres made it crystal clear that no one was to help this terrified woman and her impending baby.

She slid across the floor, backwards and forwards with the swells. The baby was released from his mother's womb. Despite her tremendous pains, she stretched out her arms and tried to reach for her newly born baby boy, but it was totally in vain. The last swell of the storm aided the mother in her pushing, tearing the baby boy together with cord and afterbirth in the opposite direction from the mother. Passengers starred in horror, no one could help. The baby smashed straight into a splinter protruding from an old salvaged wooden panel,

– Wooden panels were salvaged from the original Lady. RMS Lady from 1940 to 1946 saved and witnessed the death of many a soldier during the Second World War. She, herself was shelled by the Nazi's. This, then outdated Lady was broken down for scrap, despite her saving many an earthling throughout the world during that sacrificial war–

his mother slid across the deck to the opposite side, bashing into the ragged corner of another salvaged wooden panel.

- there were only two reclaimed panels on-board, many stories were handed down on the great deeds that RMS Lady carried out during the war. It was told that these two reclaimed wooden panels had been soaked in the blood and guts of the dying soldiers in the ship's infirmary, and were retained as a duty of respect -

At that moment of impact of mother and child, the swell ceased instantly. Passengers frantically rushed to assist the mother and her newborn baby, but it was already too late.

Everyone that witnessed this deed turned and looked towards each other as if they had lost their own child. The quietness of passengers, wind and sea was eerie, so much so that you could hear a pin drop.

Feet of the dead mother began to move, her twisted hands pulled her cold but not lifeless body to a standing position. At the opposite end the tiny baby began to move, he raised himself with his tiny and insignificant legs, twisted neck turning upwards from the ground as he rose. His head now upright, eyes opening slowly to reveal his first sight of his new life. His eyes were bloodshot, wide and glaring, sending shivers down and up the spine of the bravest.

Passengers shuffled slowly backwards, while continually starring at the mother and child with bone-chilling fear. They surrounded themselves in a circle in the middle of the deck. Looking at each other with bewilderment and despair.

Mother and son began opening their mouths wider than humanly possible, with blood dripping teeth they leapt towards the surrounded passengers and began to feed in a frenzy of thirst and hunger. I was powerless to help as they ripped only a little flesh from the passengers in a bloodthirsty massacre, but just enough to take their earthly life.

- I questioned my own beliefs as the chosen one-

Passenger bodies lay lifeless on the deck, swishing around in a stream of warm red blood until they themselves turned and awakened to their new life. I escaped, I could have secured the watertight doors, but in a panic, I forgot or did I?, as I ran for help. Frantically making my way to the captain and crew, as I explained what had just occurred. The captain ordered that I be taken and locked in a cabin.

- They thought I was crazy and that I had developed the fear of the Deads sickness-

I initially feared for the Manx people whom would soon feel the welcoming wrath of the lady of Mann and the Manx Ship of Zombies. Now locked in my cabin with a ship full of the Cruising Deads bound for Douglas Harbour, I was able to safely meditate and recalled my divine purpose. I became calm and collected my thoughts. My gift from the Divine Gods includes the power of visual communication from the past and present.

I can recall every passenger as they boarded the vessel – quiet and chatty.

I can recall their facial expressions as we set sail - happy and excited.

I can recall what they looked like when their facial expressions changed as the first swell hit the ship – concerned and frightened.

I can recall their faces as the woman and her child slid uncontrollably around the deck – powerless and shocked.

I can recall their faces as they individually turned to become flesh-eating Deads – reborn and nightmarish

I recall the feeling to join the mother and baby in the feeding but resisted. The Lady would make her final bid in history, she would be known as the boat that infected the Manx people from the Cruising Deads.

My name is Eel-Divad, I was born from the reproduction rights of original Deads, and I'm from a birth line of a chosen one. Petre has ordered me not to

interfere or harm these Deads or Zombies as the Manx
call them, but to wait for further instructions.

Manx Log 4 Tractors of Douglas Beach

Traditionally tractors could be seen on Douglas beach clearing away the masses of washed-up seaweed. This was a tidal ritual not only to provide holidaymakers with a lovely golden beach but to act as a generation of biomass power. Power supplies to the Island had been severely disrupted when America fell to the Deads and European countries took control of commodities bound for the Island.

Since European Military took control on the British and European shores, masses of decaying bodies are washing up on Douglas beach along with the seaweed. Tractors clear both from the beach, trucks take everything to the biomass power plant. Earthling's bodies and seaweed are combined to power the Island's regeneration power plant.

Decaying bodies are unrecognisable, most of the outer flesh has been eaten by the sea creatures. At the beginning, the Manx made an attempt at collecting information for families, but this was virtually impossible to do. Bodies are blessed by a priest at the biomass plant while being reprocessed to supply the much-needed power for the Islanders. At first, islanders rebelled as such outlandish deeds made people sick to their stomach. But then with the continual demise of America and the dastardly deeds of the Europeans, it became a reality in order to maintain life on the Island, sacrifice's had to be made regardless of the morality of those deeds.

Manx Log 5 My Thirst

The islands of Europe are falling and the Lady of Mann has berthed in Douglas harbour, a massive crowd of cheering and unsuspecting earthlings have gathered to welcome the ships return. They are here to celebrate the last journey of this fantastic ship that has assisted the Manx people in many a crossing, a ship that holds a tradition of mystery and magical indulgent. The Manx are sad to see it disappear yet again. This ship provided the Manx with a sense of family and security against the world.

Hundreds of welcoming earthlings are secured in the compound held tight by a stainless steel wired fence. As the doors opened on the ships worn out weary deck, the cheering crowd soon turned into a screaming mob unable to escape. The Deads disembarked quickly and with an impending need, they began a feeding frenzy on the trapped earthlings.

I escaped my confinement and stood on the open deck, watching in despair as the earthlings fell and turned. As I initially watched in horror, the sight of this turning massacre made clear my birthright. I felt the urge for the second time, the need to join in this frenzy of tearing flesh. The thirst for earthling's blood became overwhelming and it totally consumed my earthly thoughts.

I managed to resist the temptation, my purpose came to me as I recalled a vision of the divine gods.

- I was told to help, whom? And to await the arrival of the chosen one. The Manx shores will form part of the saviour of the earthlings, or so I was told -

I await news and my orders from Irish Shores, both Ireland and Isle of Man have fallen simultaneously to the Deads. Petre will be in communication soon.

Manx Log 6 Before the Deads, Tynwald

In the early days, before the Deads arrival on earth. The Island was poor in wealth, homes could be bought cheaper than anywhere else in the United Kingdom. Those that sold their homes in London were able to buy several houses in the Isle of Man from their sale proceeds.

The Manx land while poor in individual wealth was rich in Celtic and Historical Traditions. The landscape of the Island changed little over the years. Sure there were some developments that assisted the Manx people, but not that many.

Other nationalities started to arrive on the Island, work permit allocation became a requirement as many came to look for work and a safe place to live. The Isle of Man was known for its safety and little crime as compared to other countries. In those days you could leave your car door unlocked and safely return without any missing items.

People who were not born in the Isle of Man were known locally as "come-overs" and unless they possessed the wealth to purchase low priced property or start a business, they would be frowned upon.

The Isle of Man is an independent nation, but the government was called the "Wally Dog". As each year it mimicked the United Kingdom's budget. It was tied to the United Kingdom for defence and a taxation called VAT. The other ties were rarely mentioned.

While it believed it was a free nation, the United Kingdom ensured that the Manx government adhered to its laws.

Tourism and tax avoidance was its largest income producer, and then the Internet gambling institutions took hold and from a distance these gambling institutions began to destroy the morality of millions around the globe. The government turned away from its people allowing a huge disparate between income and property prices. It became virtually impossible for a normal Manx worker to be able to afford a house. Food was controlled in such a manner to protect the home producing markets, and some food became more expensive than mainland UK.

The government during the first attacks of the Deads on American soil realised that the UK Military would soon take control of the Manx lands, without authority.

So, they set about designing an underground laboratory to protect their nation.

The laboratory would design prop-packs, not operated by jet propulsion but rather by the older tradition of the propeller. The day the Deads appeared in America all jet propulsion had stopped overnight throughout the world.

Prop-packs would fit comfortably on the back of an earthling and could fly through the sky for a two-hour duration. The fuel was manufactured utilising the bodies and seaweed gathered from the beaches surrounding the Island. The mixture of bones and seaweed made high grade fuel, even cars ran on this new human fuel.

Manx Log 7 The Playground

"Miss… Miss… please Miss,… Miss Quayle", Docy screamed, "There is a Zombie", pointing with her finger stretched out, hand moving backwards and forwards with a ferocity of impatience. "Don't be silly Docy, there are no Zombies here", as Miss Quayle turned she felt the blood trickle down her neck, children ran around the playground in every direction, screaming with fear. Docy turned and shouted at Miss Quayle. "I told you so…you did not listen, you never listen to me".

Docy ran as fast as her small legs could carry her, she jumped for the mesh fence that surrounded the school and began to climb. She reached the top only to be pulled back down by Deads, she fell to the ground, turning to face her captor. It was Miss Quayle, now a Zombie, covered in blood and her neck torn, blood dripping skin hanging loosely off her torso, displaying her tendons and bones for all to see.

Miss Quayle was once a proud woman, she would cover and hide her slender young body in an old womens clothes, as if not to distract the male teachers. Now she did not care.

Docy, unfrightened, looked straight into her eyes, Miss Quayle grunted many times at her, she turned around without harming Docy and ran towards another child.

Docy quickly ran to another fence closer to the forest, doing somersaults all the way there. She stopped for a brief second, looking around towards the playground, Miss Quayle was still feasting on that unfortunate child. The majority of children were turned by the hungry Deads. Only a few like Docy managed to escape.

As she reached the woods, she began to scale a tall and straight pine tree with protruding branches. Docy climbed to the highest point and sat on two thick branches joined together, it formed a platform where she could lie down and rest without fear. Docy sat pondering and trying to make sense of what had just occurred. Her parents had assured everyone that there could be no Zombies on the Isle of Man. Docy had just turned eleven, she was a top gymnast and extremely quick and agile on her feet and climbing that old pine tree was a doodle for her.

As she drifted off to sleep her head was filled with questions. "Why did Miss Quayle not consume or turn her? How could she understand what the Zombie Miss Quayle had said when she had grunted at her? What did Miss Quayle mean when she grunted "Hold hands and run with Fellia?" How did the Zombies get here? Will my family be safe?"

She awoke with no answers to her questions, the bright stars and clear skies lit up her pathway as she climbed back down towards the ground. She heard a rustle at the bottom near some bushes and instantly stopped, out of the bush came one of her friends. Docy whispered "stay there, I will come help you", "tha...nks Do...cy" she said with a frightened stutter. Docy took her young friend by the hand and headed towards home, "stay close to me, you will be OK".

Docy was known for her boundless enthusiasm in all that she does, her smile was as infectious as the American Deads turning of America. Every child wanted to be with her, Docy was indeed a special and gifted child. She could not wait to get home as her father had been away and was returning that afternoon on the Lady of Mann with her uncle.

They reached the edge of their village, the stars in the sky disappeared as they got nearer to the bright flames of the burning petrol station. They continued their journey towards Docy's home, quietly and with an objectivity of remaining unseen. The village was deserted, abandoned vehicles were unusually parked in every direction. They could not find one person, not even a Zombie. At last, they reached Docy's home, the door was wide open, the family pet had escaped or perhaps it was released to go fend for itself, or at least that's what Docy had decided.

Her mother or father where not at home and more importantly for Docy, no bodies were found, so there was still hope in her heart. As they were leaving the house, Fellia screamed and grabbed onto Docy pulling herself close to her body. "Its OK Fellia, it's only my pet lizard," Fellia's small eyes looked up at Docy and smiled, she said "Can we go to my house now? I will be six tomorrow and we need to plan my birthday party, all my friends are coming, will you come to Docy?"

Manx Log 8 Two into One

I disembarked the ship later that night and walked straight past some of the Deads who were still feasting on earthlings. As I walked, Petre communicated telepathically and informed me that she was in trouble and that our communications will cease shortly. Immediately afterwards my connection with Ireland was severed.

My home was not far away, we need to get there quick to help the children. The divine Gods had provided us with two special powers, the power of visual recognition and the power to become two or one. I began to run and as I did my body tore and split into two separate earthlings. As one person, I was female. I became two individual males when separated, we were brothers Eel and Divad.

We began to search for Eel's daughters. Docy and Fellia were alone on this small island but we knew that they would be safe. Now it was time to find them and provide answers to the many questions that played within their soul's. While Fellia was still too young, time dictated that we informed her of her birthright. Neither knew that they were sisters, now both would have to become "one" to help save the realm of earthlings.

Manx Log 9 Sisters

For their own safety the girls were unaware that they were sisters.

Docy and Fellia travelled to the home of Fellia. They were friends since Fellia was born. They finally reached the town of Peel after many hours of walking and talking. Fellia was a wee chatterbox which went down well with Docy. While Fellia chatted away, Docy would be doing front flips and cartwheels along the grass verge of the roads. Neither thought it was strange that not a car nor person passed by them in their entire journey.

They turned the corner onto their street, full of fun and enthusiasm only to be greeted by a group of Manx Zombies. They did not touch Docy but grabbed Fellia, one began to bite her in the neck. Docy was quite small and petite but she pushed the Deads to the side and grabbed Fellia, lifting her up and began to run.

Fellia dropped to the ground with blood dripping from her neck. Docy grabbed her hand and began to run, Fellia's little legs ran as fast as they could.

Docy fell to the ground, and Fellia followed, neither of them could see each other. They screamed in excruciating pain as their bodies joined and became one for the first time. Not knowing, they shouted for each other, they were now one. They could hear each other's screams, but yet they sounded as one. "Docy! Fellia! Where are you?" Their bodies were undergoing a dramatic and life changing transformation.

We arrived on the children's transition to their birthright.

"You are all right, its dad and uncle Divad, relax be as one. You and Fellia are joining as one, don't fight it"

Docy and Fellia now accepting their birthright had become one, they became a boy in their new form. The divine gods would now provide them with special powers when joined as one to help save the realms.

Like your father and uncle, you will learn how to be one, yet you are still two, your thoughts will become one when joined together. You will be protected as one.

Docy interrupted and said, "But Fellia was bitten, I tried to save her Dad!"

We explained that Fellia is OK, "you saved her by running with her, your sister has not fully developed her powers but you saved her Docy, you saved your wee sister".

"Watch us", Eel and Divad ran together holding hands, as they did they became one, and known as Eel-Divad. Fellia-Docy now understood, while still young they instantly connected with their birthright and they knew what had to be done.

Manx Log 10 Fairy Bridge & Mythic Figures

Fairy Bridge is full of myths and superstitions for both locals and tourists. It was common practice for people to keep the fairies informed and to ask them questions. Even denying basic good manners of wishing the fairies 'good morning,' could see you receive some bad luck.

This was a daily ritual for many of the believers as they crossed back and forth over the bridge on their daily travels. Some even claimed that they had seen and had actually spoken to the fairies. Over decades true birth Maxie's told stories of impending wraths if the fairies were not taken seriously.

They claimed the fairies created drawings of unearthly images and writing's that nobody could understand. Many scientists and scholars have taken these writings to try and decipher their meanings, but none have come forward with a solution.

Since the Deads arrival in America, many scholars and anthologist have made frequent visits to the Manx Museum to try and uncover the mystery behind the writings, they believe that these writings hold an answer to the current worldly troubles.

'Manannan in Man' is another mythical tale that many books have spoken about. There are many other mythic figures originating from the Irish and Scottish shores. Now, as can be witnessed they are not as mythical as earthlings originally thought. These mythic figures are all part of the universal realms that make up all that we see.

And what we don't and cannot see is far beyond our best attempt at any form of imagination.

As a chosen one, we understand that bridges hold a special power and together with the chosen ones will form the salvation for all of the earthlings as laid down by the Divine God's.

The Manx believe that the curse of the Zombies was sent to plague them, to teach humanity a lesson in respect, respect for their fellow mankind and for the mythical creatures of this universe.

Manx Log 11 Earthlings in Hiding

The majority of the worthy Manx Earthlings were now turned, whereas the evil earthlings had been consumed by the Deads. Any living earthlings were now in hiding with limited resources to assist them.

Transmissions from the Island ceased. The Deads had turned the people who manned the radio stations on the Island including the police and national guards.

The remaining earthlings would now feel alone and terrified.

We are awaiting the divine god's intervention as all communications have been lost with the chosen one Petre. We managed to save only a few of the Manx earthlings, this was remarkable due to our overwhelming urge to feed and turn them.

The children have spoken with the divine god's,

they have informed us that we all need to run together and become a united one. We separated from each other and the four of us ran together for the first time, all four becoming one. The surge of power was overwhelming and provided the power to reconnect with the Divine God's and the chosen one in Ireland.

As commanded, we sought out the remaining earthlings on the Island.

We came across a young lad, who was not hiding, but paying respect to his young dead mother. He needed her, he wanted to be held by his mother and told that everything will be OK. Earthlings bring life into earth and then they turn to addictions that ruin their's and their children's life's. Her gravestone read

- Died so young at the hands of drugs and alcohol, Sorry to my Children, RIP age 33 -

In the moonlit graveyard, the lad at first began kicking and screaming, trying frantically to pull his foot away from the hand that obviously came from the ground to secure his destiny. Relaxing and accepting his fate, he calmed down and looked downward towards his captor. He became at ease when he seen the overgrown grass tangled around his ankle, he felt such a fool, he knelt down to free himself.

His eyes began to fill with tears of joy while they turned towards his right shoulder and then to his left.

His eyes changed colour to that of a lifeless shade of grey and yellow as the two Deads sunk their teeth into either side of his neck. Slowly, as if not to harm, but only to turn him. Maybe the Deads felt compassion for this lonely boy who lost his mother? That surely was torture enough, witnessing a mother shrink and suffer at the hands of earthling-made addictions.

Falling onto his hands as the Deads released their grip, he smiled towards his mother's tombstone, content in the knowledge that they would soon be together again, or so he thought?

Most of the hidden locals were located in two separate locations both known as the fairy bridge. One on Castletown road known by the transport travellers and the other, some claim is the real fairy bridge at Kewaique. The search continued until there was no one left to be found.

Turning each earthling into a Deads was our birthright. While we resisted at first, the overpowering desire of our four souls combined as one, compelled us to be a juggernaut in the turning of the remaining earthlings on the Island.

The transformational turning of the last earthling on Manx soil ended with a united howl of grunts from all that had been turned.

The Isle of Man had succumbed and now became

the Isle of Deads.

Manx Log 12 Avro Lancaster

The last transmission from the Island was met in London with an immediate order. To scramble the re-commissioned Lancaster four-engine Second World War heavy bombers to totally destroy the Isle of Man and its inhabitants.

Deep underground, the earthlings of the secret development bunker listened to each communication sent by London to the Lancaster Bombers.

They prepared themselves, the only four remaining earthlings on the Isle of Man. They rose to the surface with the Prop-packs in hand, unknown what they would or could do to stop the bombers, but at least they were going to try. After all they had a right to live as well and no one from Europe were going to murder them.

The bunker doors opened and the two woman and

two men were met by Eel, Divad and the children.

"Ten Minutes to drop," vibrating from the rusty speaker that they held in their hands.

Eel raised his hands in the air and the Deads that were charging to the hilltop stopped and turned away.

The scientists understood their fate while the children helped get the prop packs onto their backs, Eel explained what their new life would be like.

Prop packs were light and could reach speeds faster than the Lancaster.

"The pilot of the Bomber can be distracted, on their arrival, fly directly in front of them." Divad turned to Eel and asked him to demonstrate how to crash the aircraft.

"When the pilot sees you, he will bank to the starboard side, the others need to push the rising wing upwards until the aircraft stalls. The pilot will try and correct this by pulling up. If he does then you need to continue your push upwards. The aircraft will stall and enter a spin to the sea below."

These 'old timers' are the same as our grandfathers would have flown during the Second World War. Now they are being used to kill their own kind.

As the final aircraft disappeared into the Irish Sea, the scientists landed and removed their prop-packs, they knelt before us and asked: "Will it hurt?" As the last earthling turned, we now await orders from the new chosen one and Divine God's.

Our Fairy Bridge will form one of the Bridges for the salvation of earthlings, the Realms and Deads.

Manx Log 13 Writings of the Deads

On earth, the Deads communicate with grunts. Their grunts can be understood by the Chosen Ones.

In their own realm, the Deads also have writings.

Your Earthling ways have jeopardised the universal realms and you are facing an extinction greater than that of the Dinosaurs.

We come from the realms of the Deads, we are here to help Earthlings.

Do not judge us by our appearance or by what we do to you. For what we do to Earthlings is for all Earthlings.

Volume 1 The Chosen One

My hand written logs of my journey

Log (-1) 1984 Top Secret ZOMBIES

The Year 1984, February 29th, Time 23.59 Isle of Man

In the year 1,000, Deads came to earth, but their plans to turn earthlings were curtailed, by a Chosen One from my bloodline. Our treaty included forty Deads remaining in secret on earth.

In 1984, a fracture became visible above fairy bridge, on the Isle of Man ten days before February twenty-ninth.

This fracture, resulted in a world meeting, with Ronald Reagan, George Bush, Bill Clinton, Margaret Thatcher, Li Xiannian, Indira Gandhi, Sultan Ali Keshtmand, Saddam Hussein, Pierre Mauroy, Erich Honecker, Konstantin Chernenko and many other leading politicians and leaders throughout the world, they sat at a special security meeting with my team.

For some leaders, this was the first time they had been at the same table together. This time changing event was wasted, as each had their own agenda and no one could see eye to eye, well they pretended they did. Only for the record.

Each political leader had travelled to Douglas in the Isle of Man in absolute secret.

The realm of Deads, with the help of those left behind, began chipping away at the fracture, at either side. Using their razor sharp fanged teeth, in an attempt to invade earth.

My team agreed on a settlement with the remaining Deads, that roamed Earth. They in return, convinced the realm of the Deads, that earthlings with immediate effect, will change their ways towards the planet and themselves.

To bind that union the following were agreed:

A) A Manx 1984, Sovereign Coin, with the image

of the Queen's head, transformed into a Deads. Was minted by the Treasury, to act as a reminder to all earthlings, of what could occur on earth.

B) The Deads would sit on the world leaders council.

C) The remaining Deads could travel freely around the earth.

One minute later, Earthling leaders, on misguided advice from their military, reneged on their arrangement with the remaining Deads.

The military disbanded my team and informed us to remain silent, under mysterious circumstances, five members of the team have since disappeared. Earth leaders had no intention of making a deal with Deads.

I have no idea, what happened to the forty remaining Deads on our planet, but I pray that they are, safe, free, and well treated for the sake of earthanity.

I have the only remaining Sovereign coin as proof of the agreement.

Log (- 0) Below Ground Zero

The Year 1999, Friday, 31st December at 13:00, California.

    Crage, my Irish friend for many years, arrived at San Francisco International Airport from London Gatwick for an extended holiday. We drove to Mountain View Centre for Performing Arts, to attend the conference, 'Our Environment.' On the way there Crage kept me up-to-date with my family in London. Explaining in great detail, how they loved every moment of their school trip. The Tower of London,

Madam Tussaud's and the Dungeons became their favourite haunts to visit.

"They told me to give you hugs and kisses, and they can't wait until they return in a weeks time." Crage threw her two hands around me, and we embraced.

I looked into her eyes, we both had tears of happiness streaming down our faces, and I said "Crage, It's been way too long. But, I'm so glad you're here now."

One of the hero's on Rainbow Warrior, she put her life at risk on the high seas for over fifteen years trying to stop, countries, companies, and misguided officials from destroying our environment. Without brave earthlings like Crage, our planet stood little chance of surviving. She and her colleagues saved many an earthling, by highlighting the dangers of misguided officials in their attempts to dominate others.

After her speech, we went looking for food; many excellent restaurants lined the streets. Since she loved Spanish food, we chose patio seat's at the Cascal Restaurant. The startled waiter dropped his tray, as the lone black wolf bit into Crage. She laughed the incident off, "I'm all right, he is only hungry, look how skinny he is."

"That's strange, wolfs usually travel in packs and never do they enter a busy town. Crage, are there any in Ireland?"

"No! Irish history states that the last remaining wolf died sometime during 1786 and Black wolfs are rare in America. He looked to single us out for some reason? Petre, talk to the Wolf!"

After the bite, he rested his head on my lap. Despite what occurred in our family tree, we still loved wolfs. Holding the majestic fluffy beast in my arms, I looked into his gold and black eyes and asked, "Why, did you bite her?"

Our brief encounter took me on the journey of the wolf's existence, only three months old when they snatched him from Yellowstone Park. Now two years old and just escaped from the genetic research unit at Stanford University.

He told me to remain with my friend, and the unanswered questions to 1984 will become apparent. His ears pointed straight as he lifted his head to howl. He knew what was about to befall him. His blood splattered across my face, the bullet exiting his head and grazed my shoulder, on its way to finally lodge in the tree standing behind. The force of the impact knocked me from my seat; the wolf fell on top of my leg.

Crage jumped from her seat screaming "Petre are you OK, Petre...?"

The officer ran towards Crage, "Don't move, get on the ground!" his gun firmly against Crage's head.

I shouted, "Can't you see she was bitten? YOU FUCKING FOOLS nearly killed me!"

As I pulled the dead wolf to the side, I rose to face this injustice, the butt of his Glock G43 pistol, came towards me.

My eyes opened, they were covered in blood, probably a mixture of wolf and mine. Two soldiers stood staring and kicking at me with their glossed military boots.

"Where's' Crage? What did you bastards do to her?"

Two men lifted me from the cold stone floor. "Come with us!"

No one showed any compassion or apology to what they had done.

"Where am I?"

"You are at 'Below Ground Zero' a secret unit at the genetic laboratory in Stanford."

"Why? Take me to Crage."

I struggled to free myself, but the soldiers held me tighter, pulling me along the white corridors of hell.

We entered an operating room, Crage lay on the bed, with several nurses and doctors, carrying out surgery on her.

"What the fuck are you doing to her? She only had a bite, it wasn't life threatening."

"That's our wolf, your friend is in..."

"CLAMP, Nurse, Quick... I can't stop the bleeding."

Why is this happening to her? My faith, now in the hands of her captors, made my sorrow sink deeper into the abyss of despair.

The beep... beep... of the monitor gradually became less, until the line dissolved into one continuous whine. The doctor appeared to be trying to save my friend's life. Her heart failed. Now she was dead. I sighed and slumped, the men that were holding me released their grip. The guilt of being a chosen one. Unable to keep her alive, was like gasoline in my gut, my insides dying slowly in the toxicity, needing no more than a spark to set it ablaze. My soul, now burnt out, I fell to the ground in utter despair.

The soldiers with no compassion whatsoever dragged me back to my quarters, opened the door and threw me to the floor. As they left the room, I overheard their conversation.

"She is no good to the scientist now! "What do you think, gun or pills?"

"Let's do it, it's your turn, only this time don't miss!" The trigger of their gun clicked into position.

What is this place? And how could they demonstrate so much power, especially in a busy town full of by-watchers? How would they explain our disappearance to everyone?

With seconds to spare, my encounter with the wolf entered my visions. I began scratching at the door and howling like a wolf. They took me from the room gagged and tied me to the back seat of a small airport like vehicle.

They drove me to a room, filled by the 1984 Deads. Each one strapped to tables with tubes exiting their bodies that were connected to silver tubular tanks. They in turn, were attached to a hub that powered a generator.

Pointing to the table in front of me

"Look, that's what the wolf did to your friend."

Crage lay on the bed, now turning to become a

Deads.

"Now she will be one of the chosen to power our future electricity for all earth kind."

They removed my gag. I began shouting and screaming in frustration, "You bastards! What have you done? You are abusing your powers and broken the unity that we fought to preserve. Earthanity will perish because of you."

With the ferocity and skill of an animal, the blood from the wolf began to pulsate through my entire body, providing me with the strength to knock the guards to the ground. After I had given Crage a kiss on the forehead, I released the tubes and clamps that kept all the Deads captor. The scientists tried to escape, but it was too late for them. Blood poured from the jugular, of the doctor that failed to save Crage; she gave him no chance to return as a Deads.

Five hours away from the turn of the millennium, and the actions of these idiotic scientists have started a catalyst of events that will become unstoppable. May the Divine Gods be with all Earthlings. As I ran from the building with the keys to a Military bombproof vehicle, I turned around to witness, the 1984 Deads ravaging and feeding on the remaining, evil and misguided earthlings. My chances of stopping the fracture became almost non-existent, but I had to try.

Log O Xenophobia

Sometime, after birth of earth

to Present Day

It all makes sense to Deads!

Does the following mean anything to you?

Wars, revolutions, internal conflict, battles, confrontations between each other, repression, non-acceptance of others, individualisation, colonisation, a decline of community, force of your will among others.

Blood is red no matter what earthling or animal body it originates.

Climate change, destruction, weapons of mass destruction. Fair, unfair.

Materialism, greed, intellectual, developing, undeveloped, third world, poverty, inequality.

Hunger, famine, disease, epidemics.

Leaders are deceiving their followers. And followers are so engrossed, in misdirected beliefs and traditions that they cannot see, the pure light, of earth and their existence.

Earthlings believe that their way is the only way, no respect, no tolerance. Their way or the highway.

Money is buying the best home, land, position in society, leadership of nations.

Money is buying the best legal defence, Yet the law should be equal for all!

Nationalisation then privatisation, and back to Nationalisation. Jobs suffer, running lean and profitability has its cost for Earthanity.

Why do we need charities? If earthlings worked

together, as one united force, joined as one unified nation, for our planet and the realms, then, Charities would no longer be required. But until earthling leaders see sense, these charitable foundations, give assistance and hope to where needed.

Insignificance. Millions of Earthlings slaughtered in wars and conflict. In these terms, one earthling's death is insignificant. But look into your child's eye, as they are dying or turning and tell yourself that!

Earth is a realm within an infinite universe, filled with other planets connected via the realms. The Divine Gods sit in judgement at their table awaiting each soul. Earthlings are the newborns of the universe of diversity.

Earth is the key to the realms.

and

Earthlings are disposable.

Xenophobia is defined as:

"fear or hatred of foreigners, earthlings from different cultures, or strangers. It can also refer to fear or dislike of customs, dress, and cultures of earthlings, with backgrounds different from our own."

Earthlings have turned on their own, as described in the meaning above. Now they are about to feel, the full force and true meaning of Xenophobia, towards all earthlings:

You WILL Fear The Deads

Log 1 Re-Born

The Years 1898 to 2000

Ana and Stefan, my parents, both born in Romania, from a blood line including European, Asian, and Hispanic ancestors. They immigrated to London, amidst the war and famine in their homeland, but life turned out harder to survive in the city, mainly due to the little English they spoke.

The 1st World War murdered seventeen million earthlings. My father couldn't enlist as his one leg remaining, made him a hazard to the war effort.

His left leg torn from his body, by a wild pack of wolfs in their village. Youth shielded him from the memories of that bloody ordeal. My mother remembers each gory detail, to which I will spare you the details. In one of her many stories, she told me, not standing and fighting next to his father, and mother's father was his biggest regret.

I never met either of my grandfathers, as they both died in battle, keeping their families safe, from the madness of possessed and evil earthlings. Some believe these sacrificial wars gave the curse new meaning.

My parents, childhood sweethearts, and like many at that time hard workers, their fingers, worked to the bone, for food and a roof over their heads.

My mother fell pregnant, a sweet young lady of small build and a grafter. She cared for all earthlings that crossed her path. Mum would often be seen giving her meal to beggars in the street, and would rather go hungry herself than let someone suffer.

My father a confident, firm and fair man of short and muscular build. He would be the entertainer to the local kids and used his artificial leg as a prop.

His missing leg did not hold him back in any way.

The promised land of America was silver lined with plentiful jobs, and riches or so they were told. They managed to secure berths on a ship bound for America. A few weeks later, they packed what little possessions they had and made their way to the docks. Setting sail on a cold, cloudless day, the waters calm and peaceful. The ship berthed at the City of Derry, where they remained for several days, loading supplies before the final crossing.

My parents told many a tale of their stay in that city. My dad drank little alcohol, but the locals never saw such a happy one legged man before. So they kept buying him a pint of Guinness.

He got drunk for the first time in his life and probably his last! He made loyal acquaintances and one person in particular, 'Gerard.' Gerard would talk the hind legs off a donkey. They remained friends and in contact for the rest of their lives.

At 23.59, on the 11th November 1918, I entered the realm of earthlings in Derry. My mum took complications after my birth, and doctors fought to save her life. She lived her remaining life barren, butchered by the ships doctor. She held me tight, close to my food, her breast, and would gaze into my eyes for hours on end, thanking the gods for a wonderful and beautiful child, whispering to me;

"I will let you into a secret, all babies are a miracle, but you are a unique child, you are the chosen one."

Both my parents showered all their love, and energy into my upbringing. My parents died on our way to my twenty-third birthday party. A light aircraft ran out of fuel and collided with our car; I was the only survivor of the accident. Gerard travelled to America with his son Michael for the funeral.

In their will, I received their estate including a wealth of shares and stocks. Gerard received a document bequeathing my father's property in Ellan Vannin.

After the funeral, I joined Gerard and their family in the Isle of Man. I was part of a secret operation to keep Deads from arriving at our Realm. The Second World War claimed eighty million earthling lives, 3% of the earth's population.

The horrific number of deaths from that war were consuming the Divine Gods processing of those souls.

The wars and the dying created cracks in the fabric of the realms. While we were able to curtail this initially, the continued wars, rebellions, and revolutions throughout the world triggered a chain of events; that would ultimately result in another push by the Deads, to take control of earth.

At forty-two I died and was reborn to an American wealthy Romanian family residing in Hollywood. My name is Petre Toma.

My gifted talents proclaimed me as a child from God. At age three, I asked mom and dad how they selected my name. They told me the day they married a man befriended them and offered my father the position of a partnership in his scientific design company.

My family became quite wealthy within a short period; they asked how could they ever repay him? His answer "name your first child after me." He died peacefully in his sleep, one year later. On the day of his death, an ambulance took my mother to the same hospital his body lay. She delivered me, in a room next to the mortuary and honoured their word.

At the age of six, my doctor sent me to the hospital with a suspected brain tumour. I lay on a bed located in an old busy rundown corridor of an emergency ward. Several trainee doctors came rushing towards me; my body shook, and convulsions restricted my air intake.

The young clueless doctors panicked they turned towards each other, not knowing what to do. A senior doctor appeared, at the same time I sat up on my bed and declared, "I am fine now."

I informed the doctor, he should admit my mother

for immediate surgery as her womb contained a cancerous growth, soon to kill her. The doctor staring at me in bewilderment, a six-year-old!

"Would you check my wife?"

I grew up with a loving and caring family. At the age of twenty-two, I lost my way in life, so much knowledge and power within myself, the feelings became unbearable. My mind consumed by easing the suffering, that I believed would never end. My sleep broken as I became consumed with uncovering the reasons of my existence. I turned to the gods for assistance but got none. Desperate! My thoughts in my head insisted I had no other choice; I needed to travel and meet the Divine Gods face to face.

I jumped into my blue Ford mark one escort that my parents bought for my twenty-first birthday. Raced along the highway at the speed of 177 km/h, released my seatbelt, and drove straight into a barrier designed to keep cars from crashing into the bridge. The rounded edges of the ramp acted as a runway. Propelling the car into the air, hitting the underside of the roof. I died instantly the vehicle smashed into its bricks and iron.

The car scraped along the ceiling, exiting the bridge at the other side, destroyed beyond recognition, crushed, its parts lay scattered all around the highway in both directions.

In the instant of death, my soul passed through the realms; I sat at the table of many gods. "We have been waiting for you, our Chosen One."

They explained in the year 1,000; my family became the line for the defenders of earthlings and Deads. Our purpose to protect and to find a cure for the realms.

Explaining further, the Deads appear every thousand years, only this time they are stronger and are evolving quicker, a direct result of earthling atrocities. The cure can only come from a bloodline within my family tree, past, present or future.

The treaties between the Divine Gods and the other realms do not allow the Gods intervention.

At their table of wisdom, we spoke what appeared to be forever. On my death I received the answer I needed, I was not insane. The gods told me this was part of their plan; I needed to pass through the channel of an earthlings death and return if indeed I was the chosen one!

At the end of my divine meeting, distant shouting, and screaming became louder.

Dim lights became bright. My mother's screams of joy and my father's cry, "she is alive."

Despite the destruction of my vehicle, I lay on the hospital bed; my body had no internal or external injuries. The earthlings who witnessed my body being cut free from the wreckage, proclaimed it's a miracle.

Many years have passed, it is now 2016, and the Deads have walked on our earth, ravishing and turning for sixteen years. I am the chosen one; my job is to take the earthlings to Europe and find a cure.

Deads, are becoming harder to send back to their realm. These are my logs. In the event I turn or be killed, my research can be used to find my next in bloodline.

My path of finding a cure will only take me so far, the application of healing is down to the pure fight for earthanity. The willingness of earthlings to accept equal rights for each other. The Gods are disgusted at the new earthanity, where religion and local ownership have become more important than earthlings themselves. At this time the world should be reuniting. Instead, they are breaking apart from each other. This way forward is not Gods will, but the evils of individuals in power. Those who prey on the insecurities of the Earthling race, to further their goals and plans at any expense, by making false claims and creating havoc throughout the world of earthlings.

My research traced the originating dead on American soil to a man named as Torber Kimrank.

Torber was not bitten by a Deads but turned to a Deads. He is not the first in history, but he is the one responsible for the mass Deads outbreak in America. His bite originated on earth. I believe he is now one of the leaders of the Deads, but this cannot be confirmed or denied.

Torber, a wealthy and articulate man, he loved to put his wealth on show and dressed to impress. While he loved the ladies, many a male guest was seen leaving his bedroom with a smirk. He amassed most of his wealth from business acquisitions, within the news and print industry, and owned many properties overseas, including the Tonhil Group of Hotels. Every weekend, guests would arrive from all around the globe to be at Torber's mansion parties in Hollywood. The parties were full of personalities and politicians. Despite the accusations thrown at him when some guest disappeared, the parties never stopped, and neither did the earthlings attending them. They came from around the globe for his lavish extravagance.

Torber came from deep European roots, his ancestry traced back to the year 1,000, and consisted of Scottish, Irish and Croatian descent. One of his ancestors, the Croatian Jure Grando, died in 1656 and became a vampire. The first Deads are referred to as Zombies by modern earthlings. My logs will make no reference to the term Zombies. Hollywood produced Zombie films until 2000. Zombies are fictional characters as opposed to the Deads.

Log 2 The Deads Arrive

The Year 1999, Friday, 31st December at 23:59:50. Around the bridge of Sixth Street Viaduct

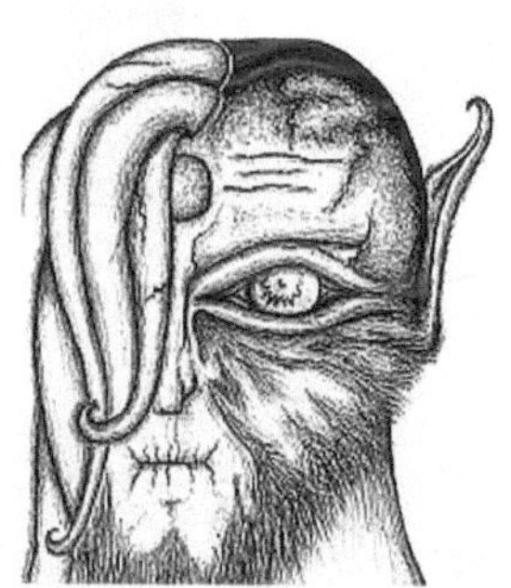

I arrived too late! What was about to occur was now unstoppable.

Hogmanay is a Scottish tradition; some say derived from the Anglo-Saxon days. Earthlings partied in the streets of Hollywood, to welcome the new millennium in real Scot's style. The clear night soon changed, first with a smither of rain, then became quite foggy. The gathering crowd of earthlings were in a joyful mood, parties raging. Despite the temperature dropping to -1 centigrade from its usual 9, everyone continued to dance, not noticing the sudden coldness.

The pipe band stopped playing, and the countdown began, 10. 9. 8. 7. 6. 5. Silence, then 4 - 3 - 2 - 1. The president shouted, "Happy! New Year!" Earthlings hugged, kissed, and linked arms to sing, Auld Lang Syne.

Then the New Year started with a brilliant display, crackling loud bangs, smoke filled the skies, from the exploding fireworks. Fog masked the opening of the Deads realm, they came through a crack in the sky above Sixth Street Viaduct, on that cold and smoky ten seconds.

Deads appeared, and everyone cheered them on, I witnessed the first horrific and tragic attack. Next, the bloodthirsty creatures rampaged through the crowds, ripping flesh and bones and spitting them to the ground.

Bill Clinton and his family, with vice president Al Gore, stood on the open air stage toasting the earthlings. They toasted the release of a new horror film, "New Years Horrors," some of Hollywood's famous directors and actors were on the stage, shaking hands with Bill.

The Deads landed on the stage and began tearing flesh from the presidential party, again spitting the body parts to the ground. This ritual repeated itself many times. Bystanders filmed and cheered unaware they were playing the part of extras, in a real and terrifying tale.

Too late for Bill, Al and Arnold Schwarzenegger. Hilary and her daughter Chelsea fell from the stage and landed next to where I stood. Helping Hilary to her feet, I beckoned them to follow me. I created a pathway through the cheering crowds to their helicopter. Chelsea shouting "MY DAD, my dad, please help him," but he had turned, just like the others.

They asked me to join them, but earthlings needed saving. The drone of the blades made parts of our conversation rotate into the abyss. I shouted, "HILARY, the nation will need your leadership." My emotions displayed tears and happiness, as they disappeared in shock into the night sky.

I returned to the ongoing massacre, only able to help a few more escape. As the chosen one, I was powerless to save them, and a tremendous sense of discouragement took hold of my soul.

Minutes later the president's party turned to Deads, dropping to their hands and knees and consuming the discarded blood and flesh, like a pack of starving hyenas. Their heads lifted from the ground; grayish glowing piercing eyes now turned to a predator as they searched for their next victim. Kindergarten Deads, learning for the first time, how to feed on a planet rich in earthlings and plumb for the taking.

Once finished they attacked others with the same repeating ritual. The masses realised too late; many became infected and they re-infected thousands more. Deads turned the majority of our military within days. Gun lovers got no time to use their vast armoury.

The administration destroyed, Hilary did not take command, but another strong leader took the role as commander-in-chief.

Barrack Obama faced difficulties in trying to lead through these troubles. Without an infrastructure, America's protection and freedom of rights, are now history.

Mexico, South America, and Canada fell next. Eight hundred and fifty million earthlings were now Deads. With only a few million earthlings remaining in the Americas. Europe and the East were the only countries unaffected.

American military based in Europe and the

Middle East remained there and joined the European army.

Bill had attended Oxford University in England, and was a member of a select group investigating the "Deads of 1,000 BC," an international governmental operation uncovering the details of their existence. Clinton, an important ally for the Deads to turn. He was also one of the 1984 team members, on the Isle of Man; the Deads will certainly not forget about that traitorous night!

I tracked and discovered some of the originating Deads. I confirmed the small bites found on their necks, similar to a bat's bite originated from planet earth. Bloodline Deads do not leave bite marks on their victims. They tear away whole body parts and communicate with grunts, and weird noises, filling the body with chills.

From the first attacks on American soil, I established communication with our European partners. Europe is in lock down and at the moment, free from Deads. These are strong allies who believe in what I say, and whom I say I am. The answer to our prayers is rooted in history, attempting to convince the cruise earthlings to set sail is my biggest challenge.

Log 3 Hunters

The Year 2001 - American Soil

During the first year of the Deads entering our realm, Earthlings were still running lost to find help. They were coming together for protection against Deads and earthlings.

Fraternities were groups of earthlings, joining with a common purpose, utilising existing buildings and or re-enforcing them. The first that I joined, turned out to be a hell hole, full of misguided and evil earthlings.

After a month we managed to escape, it was a fraternity of mental and physical torture. If such a term exists it was a 'hell hole of horror.'

Their Hunters found us before we could escape their boundary. They separated us and after twenty minutes of Mirror screaming; she was brought back to where I stood. They forced Mirror to the ground, her knees landing on mud, filled with crushed pebbles, now covered in her seeping blood.

She glanced towards me, unable to cry for help. Her bright blue eyes stared in fear, awaiting her unjust fate, flesh to be torn from her body. A scene you needed to witness to comprehend the severity of the act.

Have you ever seen flesh torn from a body while it's still alive...?

He held her by the once long and beautiful blond hair. Everlasting hours would be spent brushing to perfection. His knife displayed the motive of a carved Deads head in the handle.

With the edge of his razor sharp blade, he made a cut with the precision of a surgeon. Pieces of her skin, two inches across, sliced and pulled, the blood dripping from her soft, tender face.

Hearing the sound of skin severed from a body is unthinkable!

Both of us now kneeling, they are demonstrating a ritual of power in the community, of only masculine and testosterone bullshit. The world, unknown to the earthlings, faced an extinction parallel to the dinosaur age.

Torn skin from an earthling makes a noise; I will never forget.

Parts of her flesh hung from her face, with the ferocity of a cheetah, he pulled downward with his thumb and index finger; blood splattered into my mouth, and her flesh landed on my arm. They had sealed her mouth with stitches made from dirty cotton. Each groan oozed blood from between the gaps in her lips.

Have you ever felt warm blood from an earthling splatter against you?

Bitten and turned would be a wish for compassionate salvation.

I await my torture, pain I will endure, like life itself will soon be over. To kill your wife, husband or friend, turned by Deads, would be a personal choice.

Have you ever wished to be bitten and turned?

We were weak, starved of food and water, confined in darkness for weeks before our escape. I put everyone's life at risk telling the leaders my purpose, a bad idea. Now we are dying at the hands of earthlings without compassion. I prayed to be turned, to seek revenge against their misdeeds on their own kind.

Would you want your dead wife or husband turned by a DeadS, so that they may walk on this earth again?

Whenever earthlings Turn, families and friends slaughter their loved ones. Some keep the DeadS locked in rooms, while others decapitate and smash their heads to a pulp. Do you possess the skill set required to murder?

Are you afraid to reach out and touch another? Not scared to bring life into this new world of mistrust and horror?

On my travels, I found many earthlings places of abode. Babies are still being born, earthlings still look for comfort and the need to be with another. New life will be created, and shall rejoin a world of chaos. But can new life repopulate earth faster than the DeadS are destroying Earthanity?

An encounter of being chewed horrifically, by one once living is disgusting. Earthlings munch away on a Sunday roast dinner, and are remarkable for justifying their actions, seeking redemption to their Gods for animal sacrifice.

Have you ever encountered an uncooked earthling being chewed?

My friend and I witnessed our captors taken by surprise, receive justice. Each one consumed by a herd of Deads.

Mirror was the only one Turned to join the Deads, and as I fell to the ground, she smiled, her torment stopped. I awoke alone several hours later.

Would you murder your family if they turned to a Deads?

This horror and it's choices, is the new world we now live in, and I am the Chosen One to lead all earthlings to freedom. My name is Petre Toma. I will take you through a somewhat unusual and chaotic journey with my writings of these horrific events and my travels to the Cruise Ships.

Finding a cure from Deads is my birthright.

Log 4 Evolution

The Year 2005, USU Energy Research Centre, Bingham.

This facility was vital to our national security. Initially, they were developing sensors to be used in space missions. We discovered that they could be used to disguise an earthling from Deads. The environmental interaction with the RF optical signals created an interference with the Deads internal sensors, and any earthling wearing a sensor became a

Deads in the eyes of Deads.

The sensors required a trigger from a satellite in space. At this stage, I have no idea why our sensors failed. They had protected me on my travels for three years

Everyone at the research institute was taken by surprise, and our research and sensors destroyed.

Jonah, and I were the only two to escape, I turned around to speak to him and was met with muscle and blood splattering across my face and mouth, torn and ripped from an earthling by the razor sharp teeth of Deads. I stood, blood dripping from me, the Deads gripped my friend with two clawed hands, no chance of his escape, I was helpless to help, his fate had been decided. They turned and peered straight into my eyes while they Deads tore away another part of the flesh. Should I kill Jonah and the Deads, or run to safety? These are a few erratic decisions my possessed mind tried to answer within a split second.

The blood trickled down my throat and into my stomach. I raised my fists towards the Divine Gods, "Why? I'm now infected, how can I help earthanity now?" I lay on the ground in despair, awaiting my fate. Jonah's eyes fading, and with his last breath, "Petre RUN! You ARE the chosen one; please RUN!". His enthusiasm for my faith jump-started my adrenaline, I leaped to my feet, and took a last glance into his closing eyes, and ran until I reached a cabin at the Logan Cemetery.

I took no precaution, I discarded my checklist, and stumbled through the door. I cowered in the corner of a room filled with dust, dirt, and an empty coffin. Old dusty blackout curtains remained closed on the windows, the room in darkness, a damp and musty aroma drifted from a blast of air as I entered.

Consumed with disbelief, ashamed of myself, I let him die. Minutes and hours passed away, now ready for my turning. The memories we shared, laughter, challenges, and death. He fought like a Pit-bull to defend me; Jonah had travelled by my side for a couple of years, helping me spread the hope of the cruise ships.

I fell asleep and in my dreams the table of the gods appeared in a vision. "Petre, you can access our encounter via your memories, and you will find the answers to everything we discussed, some you need to trust in yourself."

I awoke and realised earthlings could not turn by coming into contact with Deads blood. The virus does not survive outside their body. The transfer will only occur from fluid transmission between a Deads and an earthling including a bite, intimate kissing, and sex. How can anyone contemplate either?

I departed by foot from Hollywood, California,

and I have walked through many states and towns and met friendly and evil earthlings. The war with the Deads did not make evil earthlings less evil towards their kind. These "evil to the core" earthlings continued their sadistic rituals, only now they did so with the captured Deads and earthlings.

Law and order no longer exists, and they operate how they want, albeit in the confines of their fraternity. No salvation came for the Earthlings or the Deads, the only Savior in those places, escape or be turned. In the end, these earthlings will be outsmarted. Deads are evolving and becoming wiser and smarter at an alarming rate.

Over the last four years I witnessed dramatic changes, Deads are no longer charging at fraternities if they believe they can be hurt. Leaders dismiss me as insane, so I stay quiet, learn a lot and move to my final destination of getting to Europe.

Log 5 Earthlings are Dying, Deads are Evolving

A mixture of Recapped Lost Logs covering various time spans from 2000 upwards.

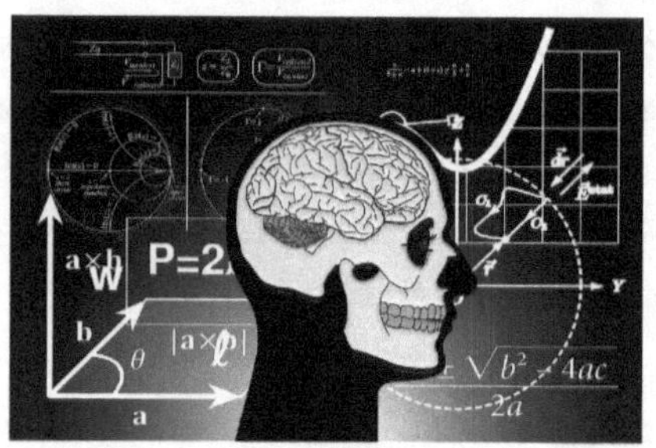

I arrived in Denver in the year 2006, and for nine years, it was my base, travelling to other states North and South informing and convincing earthlings to move to the Cruise Ships. My logs. The 'Logs of a Chosen One' were forgotten, now lost, as we rushed from our fraternity. They overpowered us while trying to seize supplies for themselves.

Americans have existed with safety on cruise ships located around the harbours of America and Canada. Cruise ship earthlings are a community of Earthlings; they communicate with each other via radio. Food and water are difficult to source. Once on the vessel, you are not allowed to leave and return due to the perceived possibility of cross-contamination.

Tug-Boat crew stood to protect earthlings, and they search for supplies needed to keep the ships operational. This service does not come cheap. A bartering system now replaces the global monetary system.

Men predominately populate tug-boats. In return for supplies, earthlings are required to provide a red light district for both male and female earthlings; these are separate secure areas of the ship and maintained in pristine medical condition. Each person visiting these quarters must remain in the containment center for three days while checks are carried out and before they are permitted to return to the decks.

No test can confirm who hosts the virus. Quarantine is the only way of detecting the disease; earthlings can turn to a dead after being bitten within minutes, hours and now days. The strain redevelops, as what can only be described as evolutionary. Possible to stop it's early detection and eradication.

The ships communication and video system link to Europe. They receive consistent but discomforting news broadcasts. The USA and Canadian administrations no longer transmit. Barrack Obama secured Alaska and saved many citizens and other nationalities. Many I met on my journey are travelling to Alaska to unite with him.

Many fraternities will not take stray earthlings into their camp, as this reduces the food availability and strays may be infected and put the others at risk. Most fraternities do not possess the necessary facilities or earthlings to operate containment units.

Who remain Christian? Earthlings perform many non-Christian deeds. Many who still practice their religious beliefs to the core, have changed their understanding to include every denomination and faith, as an equal. This ideology would be the making of our new society.

Some fraternities that accept lone wanderers are evil, sadistic or cannibals. Earthlings must be on guard from their semblance, justice from the Deads is nearer than what they think!

Deads are running out of food. Some are seen chewing at the bark of trees, feasting on the succulent woodlice, and worms which are rich in vitamins needed to sustain them. Deads can fast for months if not years without eating, they go into a zombie cationic state when not feeding or hunting for food. Animals are not safe from the earthlings or Deads. Once bitten animals can only die, the wolf is the only animal returning from their death. Some believe this comes from the werewolf folklore stories and Europe's unique depth of history.

Wolves, when caught, are either devoured, or the Deads will keep a turned wolf at their side, but this is a rare sight. Infected creatures can't re-infect another animal, but their bite is fatal, and pathogens will be transmitted to an earthling.

America and other neighbouring countries are now looking to Europe for salvation; many believe these countries will help end the Deads curse.

Medical research is yet to discover a cure or vaccination to halt the virus from spreading. No one is immune to the bite. For sixteen years the infection has been contained in blood, and bodily fluid transmission, and currently, no airborne pathogens exist.

Europe is monitoring the situation and introduced border restrictions, Europe is no longer governed, each country is ruled by their armed forces. Democracy replaced by an extremist dictatorship. The euro monetary system has ceased, barter is the only choice. This created an implemented euthanasia, for anyone older than 55 or those at a disadvantage.

Further backed up by a report, which stated the "UK population aged five hours a day but innovation lagged behind.

Mahlia Hank is the top scientist of the United Kingdom public services lab. She is a young and slender girl, who climbed the ranks faster than normal. Mahlia is recognised for her authoritative yet alluring figure and the flicking of her long blond hair, towards the chief's, who keep guard over her.

She explained, "While scientists found the 'ageing genes' we are having significant difficulty in understanding how the Deads genes develop at a rapid speed. We are trying to unlock the fundamentals of how we develop from an earthling to Deads. We should not preoccupy ourselves with mending models built for the past."

Concerns are growing over Hank's research; some believe corpses are being transported to the islands after testing. Our scientists do not understand; Deads are not from earth they come from a different realm within our infinite universe. I need to reach those scientists and explain the realms before they unleash a force that will destroy our existence.

The army transport the unfortunate to a secret central point, located in Jersey and Guernsey. The transported earthlings are unaware, of what is about to bestow them, believing they are moving to a protective place. Memories and visions of the 1st and 2nd world wars concentration camps return, these earthlings are slaughtered without question.

The tearing apart of families is sole destroying, in some cases, families won't be separated, children, mothers, and fathers are transported together to meet their fate. Earthlings suspicions are being raised as they no longer receive any communication from their loved ones. Within the first few months after the outbreak was announced in America, it is estimated that ten million European earthlings have been slaughtered, by the armies in London.

Forced labor man's industry; towns are under armed guard. Any person found lurking in the streets after curfew regardless of child, woman, man or animal, are shot dead without questions or mercy.

The military operation in Europe are masquerading as the authoritative figure; many believe this route of strict action is unnecessary. Groups of earthlings against this military intervention, hide in trepidation of their lives in different locations of the country while trying to assist others with similar views. The Manx nation is the only ones allowed to travel by ferry from Douglas to Liverpool.

UK media broadcasts live video footage of aircraft reaching the shores being shot down. Missiles are launched at planes landing on their soil. Sickening videos of the rocket impact with screams and begging for mercy, as their bodies are filmed falling from the bloodied skies.

Nuclear weapons were disbanded throughout the world and are now non-existent, done before the militia took command. The leaders of the free world including communist countries displayed concern over radicals taking power and wiping out earthanity. Jet propulsion became useless since the Deads arrival; researchers are at a loss on why or how.

The Navy patrols the waters for vessels, an almost impossible task. Ship and Boats are the safer way to arrive. Some boats managed to berth. However, they continue to broadcast pictures of earthlings being murdered and burned alive. Dramatic pictures, screaming, running, falling, and close-up imagery of the burning flesh from the dying earthlings. These types of murders are televised systematic in an attempt to curtail the vast numbers trying to arrive. Individual towns and counties are locked down, no new faces are allowed, if earthlings cannot display the necessary documentation, they are murdered. No judge or jury, justice does not exist, these forces are ruthless.

The American administration makes a regular hourly broadcast, informing citizens not to try and leave the coast. Many know these broadcasts are a deceptive ploy, of Europeans trying to stop any attempts to reach their country. The White House and Washington are under the Deads dominance.

Passenger debating on the cruise ships continues, and they vote on the last day of the month. The vote is simple and will change the lives of all earthlings. The question being voted on,

'Should we trust and await the Chosen One!'

Ships are safe at the moment and are free from any health problems. On my travels, I inform Earthlings of the ships. We need to save as many earthlings as the ships can hold.

Earthlings still possess the need to be nurtured, and loved; this is one trait the Deads cleansing will not remove. Confined to small areas, earthlings conceive, babies are born, different relationship types are catered for, without any prejudices.

Perhaps the lethal experiences witnessed by everyone, shall make earthlings more acceptable to each other, and in each other's individual beliefs.

Europeans are yet to see first-hand the wrath of the Deads. Instead, they have sacrificed their fellow earthlings. Ruthless individuals, slaughtering unaffected groups of earthlings based on prejudices and the false believe of infection.

The original Deads introduced and generated a different way of life for all earthlings on our planet. While earth's future is uncertain, the armed forces are moving forward in a ruthless and indiscriminate direction. That will enviably end with the annihilation of the earthling's way of life and to earth its self.

Many years passed since Torber's first infection of American earthlings. Now earthlings live in reclaimed property or grounds and build their own small fraternities. For the earthling in the wrong fraternity, if they leave, not many other fraternities will accept them. The only method of survival is to join with many of the other STRAYS, and forge an alliance to create their personalised fraternities. Leaders will defend and murder anyone who attempts to come into their society without an invite.

The Deads are bringing a new meaning to the world, a Deads Earthanity. The Deads never attack their own no matter how hungry they are, and they protect themselves. They run in packs, and they form a close connection with another dead, an unbreakable bond. Once the Bond is tied between two Deads, no other dead intervenes. The Deads do not differentiate between skin color, class or creed, they are accepted for who they are, despite the body parts they display. Deads are evolving, and the earthlings are joining them in vast numbers.

Deads do enjoy each other's company, and unlike Earthlings, they never turn on their kind. The Deads only concern is with consuming earthlings. Their existence is a life better than our current form of existence. The Deads main fault; 'Consuming earthlings in the most horrific and terrifying act of gore.' Earthlings look at a dead with disgust, sickness, and anxiety. Everyone should be able to live without fear, but the Deads think otherwise.

For some the Deads consume every part of their anatomy, they are eaten in a frenzy of attacking and ravaging the body with horrific torture. These dead earthlings pass through the realms and into the domain of the Divine gods for their salvation. For the other earthlings bitten, their souls and bodies remain to allow them to join the realm of Deads.

What will happen when they can no longer find earthlings to feed on? Will they kill or sacrifice each other for the good of the pack? Or will nature provide the answer?

Earthlings became used to the wants for a materialistic world, and they believed a life's worth is measured in goods and money. Deads needs on earth are temporal. The fabric of our existence and willingness to survive with flesh and bone intact gives us the right to fight and regain our dignity. If only we understood how to communicate with them, perhaps a way to stop the killing of the earthlings.

Earthanity is all about gone, yet in the midst of all the death and obliteration earthlings on both sides of the continent want a better life. Others in our communities believe Europe is rich in ancient writings and holds the answers to our prayers, salvation and protection. Original earthlings who turned without a bite are traced back to Ireland, Scotland and the Isle of Man.

Log 6 Food and Men to Avoid

The Year 2015, Kansas City

I entered Kansas City as midnight struck on the town clock. The town was deserted, everyone remaining indoors, perhaps due to the wind and rain? That's wishful thinking. As I walked down West 11th Street I passed the Mark Twain Ballroom, my husband and I attended a wedding function there, now it was empty and probably a shelter for the Deads. Over a thousand bar and restaurants lined the streets in the city, bringing back memories of the good old days. Many would travel here for a great Kansas barbecued steak. Mark Twain frequented Missouri, wonder what he would make of the place now?

I decided to look for an old friend Ramtin, he played Jazz at the Majestic restaurant, near to where I was walking. He was a famous Jazz singer and took up residence there. As I turned off West 10th Street and onto Broadway, four military attired individuals ambushed me with AK47's touching my head. After several questions, they hurled me into the back of a jeep. On my forced entrance to their fraternity, I saw a few cows and some chickens in a pen. Not eaten for a while, my instinct went out to slaughtering those animals and having a feast.

They interrogated me, and I told no one of my mission. Their leader needed medical assistance, and I offered to help despite my non-existent knowledge of medicine. While I possessed abilities to pinpoint body conditions, or thoughts of earthlings and animals I did not possess the power to heal the condition. My additional powers are limited, I am not a God or Disciple, I can't part water, nor feed the millions, I cannot turn Deads back to an Earthling. My purpose is to find a cure and save Earthanity from the opening realms. To do so, I will require help from worthy Earthlings.

They took me to my patient, I ran my hands along his body, and proclaimed its a possible lung infection. I prescribed rest, lots of steam water in his room, and that I would examine him in the morning. He in return ordered his men to make sure I was fed like a Queen.

The dining table was set to host a feast for many, yet I was the only earthling in the room. I sat humming Ramtin's song 'Blues at my window,' the song would make my solitude bearable. The meat's texture tasted tender, leaner and more like veal than beef, they served the food authentic Missouri style, barbecued.

On the way to my sleeping chamber, we passed a corridor with many cells. Hands appeared from the windows and cries of "help me." My captor said: "don't worry about them, they are harmless, they will be your breakfast." I managed to contain my sickness and horror. "Our cows and chickens are kept for eggs and milk; we don't slaughter animals here, only weak Earthlings!" I informed the guard, "Please make sure all your men stay with him tonight, come fetch me if he deteriorates. If he goes into a spasm everyone needs to hold him firm and tight to the bed. He will be harmless."

Horrified at myself, I stuck my finger into my mouth in an attempt to throw up the human remains that now lined my stomach. My hunger had driven all my reasoning to the back of my brain. Would you contemplate eating another earthling, if starving of hunger?

The bed was dirty and smelt of urine, which made the wooden chair in the corner of my cell more welcoming. After an hour or so, I left the room, on my way down the corridor I slid open each of the metal bars that secured the other rooms. Those trapped followed me to the outside door, at last, they were free from one of life's torment. "Would it be better to be eaten by an Earthling or a Deads, which would you prefer?" I returned to the leader's room, he rolled and tossed in a frenzy. His eyes alert, and now beginning to darken, his skin colour becoming chalky and his body immobile. With disgust, I glanced at his changing state, I turned around and told the others. "Press down hard, in a minute his body will shake, don't let him go until his lungs adjust, I will be back with some medication."

As I walked to the outside door, screams of hysterical earthlings crying for help from the turned leaders room, made adrenaline rush throughout my body. Should I stay and help? My hand now on the handle of the door, my decision was made. The sight of the escaping captors running away did not give me any comfort; they were moving in the direction of a Deads camp.

Log 7 Cryogenic

The Year 2015, Michigan, Grand Haven and Clinton

On my arrival in Michigan, I stayed the night on a train, dead on its tracks, 'a street car called desire.' The book and play flashed across my mind, an era of time no longer existent. As I cuddled up into a cosy corner, a young woman shouted over to me, "is anyone with you? I'm locking up for the night."

"no, only me, thanks."

"Where you headed?" She said as she closed the box car door with a thud.

"I'm heading over to the cryogenic unit at Clinton."

With an inquisitive and surprised look on her face she asked. "can I come with you? We can both be frozen together, keeping us safe from the earthlings."

"sure." I said wondering why she said 'earthlings?'

"Hi, I'm Desire, they gave me the nickname after a 'TRAIN CAR called Desire,' Yeh, right?"

"I get it; I'm Petre, a pleasure to meet you."

Desire slid a book across the floor to me, "Think you will like this book, I take the books from 'The Bookman' store on Washington Avenue, just around the corner from here. "On my free time I browse through all the books they have, and they don't ask for any cash, but I always return them."

The book was called 'Desire, The Journey we must take to find the life God offers.'

"Thanks, I will read it" As I packed it into my rucksack for another times read.

Desire said as she tucked a blanket around me, "Get some sleep, travelling to the unit will be tiring. It's a 197 mile journey, Deads surround the back routes; we will take the highway. I'm sure as hell game for it! The good news, I have a jeep it should only take us around three to four hours, if lucky."

First time in ages I feel safe, I fell asleep and entered dream mode. Recalling my dear friend Robert, he pioneered cryogenic research, an eccentric who believed in his work without a shadow of a doubt. Unfortunately, he died, his head now frozen and held in cryo storage. Yuri a cryo-biologist and our family friend, his expertise on European history made him an advisory for helping find a cure; I need him to join the cruise ship.

I heard Desire's voice, "Time to rise," I rocked back and forwards with Desire shaking me, as my weary eyes opened her happy face, in my face she said;

"Here's a' coffee for you," stretching her hand out in a horizontal position, with the coffee slopping over the side, dripping to the straw on the planks of the floor. My eyes looking at the spills, "don't worry, I can clean up later." Desire is a funny, cheery wee soul.

"Are you sure you want to come with me?" I asked,

"Sure as the air I breathe, after all, you will need me to show you the safe way and its quicker by vehicle for sure."

On our journey, Desire explained she found refuge on the stationary train after her family were killed by other earthlings raiding her home. All earthlings should be like her, happy, helpful and full of bubbly life with boundless enthusiasm. Desire managed to centre me and bring back some of the qualities hidden in my earthly body.

Gentle, yet strong as an ox, common sense prevailed and formed her judge and jury for every decision she made. Desire told me her father once a lawyer for one of the top firms became disheartened, by the unfairness of the law designed for the wealthy. Money bought the best-talking lawyer and never real justice, so he resigned and took to farming. The first attack, she remembers well, blowing the candles out on her eighth birthday cake when the announcement came. Desire insisted Deads are here to fight for the injustices of the Earthling race, while trying to jolt the earthlings back to kindness and equality.

As we walked away from the train, never to steam again, Desire pointed towards a hole in the ground fifty meters away, "in there!" Not knowing what to imagine, Inside the hole lay four men. "Now I will take you to the centre."

Pointing to the earthlings in the hole, "this is the reason I cannot join you, I'm the protector of the train earthlings. Protection not from Deads, but from those bloodsucking parasitic bastards we call earthlings."

The ships needed earthlings like her; I begged Desire to join me. On the turn of the year 2000; she received a dream from the Divine gods. She told me her mission in life was 'to save a Chosen One.'

"This is the day," she pulled me closer and we hugged, "you are the Chosen One."

Our journey began, and we did nothing but talk, neither of us recalled our trip, we stood at the gate to the genetics laboratory, oblivious on how we arrived. The first time in many years I chattered with a woman in depth on subjects involving trust and respect.

The electrified gate and fences kept everyone and anyone at bay, a good sign, someone here is still an earthling. The bell, Desire pressing with impatience and shouting "let us in, let us in, quick, please quick," turning to smile at me, "that should receive their attention."

The light above the fence began to flash red, then green, and opened. "Stay close by me, you never know," Desire took quick charge of my protection.

The door opened and Yuri, said "come, quick," he tugged me forward with his tall and slender fingers for a hug. "Petre, I'm so glad you are here, you are in time to witness the first rebirth of the earthlings in cryogenic storage." Desire, turned her head towards me scrounging up her eyes and wrinkles on her youthful face appeared. My shoulders raised in disbelief. "Come on, come on, time is of the essence here," he led the way, and we followed. The hallways lite bright and spotlessly clean. Desire with her quirky humour rubbed her finger along the wall, "he missed a bit of dust."

My children's past antics filled my wandering mind, knowing we will meet again in the realm of the souls. Her uncanny knack of reading what one thought, made me comfortable but she said something that made no sense. "Petre, they are fine."

We reached a room with glass doors; Yuri said: "Don't be alarmed, they won't hurt you." Both of us, bewildered, I could not believe my eyes, we overlooked a room filled with Deads standing, jittering from side to side, awaiting their release.

Yuri, shouted as he continued walking towards another door, "come on, keep up, these Deads, worked here, my senior assistant got sick, she turned and infected everyone else. I'm the only one left."

The door opened, and we shuffled in, observing one hundred and forty-three cryogenic bodies defrosting on individual tables.

Yuri pressed a bright red button and declared

"This is history in the making." Alarms sounded accompanied with red flashing lights. It did not give us any sense of security. Doors to the room where bodies lay opened and in walked the captors. Deads looked around before biting into the cold, lifeless bodies of the defrosting corpses. The eye of one glanced up at me, I recognised her, Yuri's assistant, Natia.

Their teeth sank into cold dead necks, making puncture wounds for drainage. Deads jumped backward grunting and spitting out the cooling fluids. As the Fluid drained from the earthling's bodies, Deads turned to the units and smashed the glass surrounding the banks of warm blood stored in individual bags. They drank from the blood bags, draining every last drop and returned. Once more their teeth entered the bodies, this time filling them with bagged blood.

Yuri jumping with excitement said, "I have been demonstrating to the Deads what they needed to do, and look, they are doing it! Deads are smarter than what you think!"

The Deads looked up towards us before one final bite into their frozen necks. With a ferocity of an earthling birth the cryo earthlings jump started their new life. The Deads stopped to observe their rising. Yuri Jumping with joy and screaming at the top of his voice, "My work, my research, Deads are evolving, Petre this is my gift to you!"

Deads began jumping at our viewing window to escape their confinement, they continued to smash the window until cracks appeared in the resistant glass.

Desire pulled me from the room.

Yuri shouted, "Run, Petre; I will stay with my newborn children. I have a lot to explain to them."

As we ran to escape the building, the alarms and lights in the corridors flashed in a circular pattern informing everyone of the impending danger.

The noise from the alarms would surely attract other Deads and undesirable earthlings. Desire gave me my directions. Tears filled our eyes, we hugged, the sadness in my eyes begged her to come with me.

"Petre, You and I will be alright, others need me, I will send as many as I can to the ships."

Desire turned around, and our hands slipped apart as she ran towards the jeep, waving as she drove away.

Log 8 Reproduction Unit

The Year 2016, Lexington, Kentucky

Another great city, once the home to over two hundred and sixty thousand earthlings. Now all that remain are a few hundred Earthlings in hiding.

There is a vital piece of historical data that I have to recover; Lexington was founded by European Americans in 1775. This land was taken from the Cherokee Indians, and I need to find a grave of a

Cherokee warrior, the soil of his grave is part of the cure. Now earthlings, like the native Indians, are being slaughtered, and their lands taken.

As I retrieved the last bit of soil from the grave of an Indian chief, a lady beckoned me to come over. I stood at the entrance reading the billboard, 'State abortion clinic of Lexington.' "Take no notice of that sign. There are no abortion clinics, left. anywhere in our great country. Every last one of the 1,683 clinics closed down; the Deads took care of that!" I had no response; I looked at her lost for words, who indeed would have the time for an abortion? The Lack of hygienic medical assistance, no phones to dial 9 1 1, nor hospitals to go to. Though, I'm certain some still went on.

Would you want to bring life into a country whose population of Deads exceed that of earthlings? The women who lived during the world wars, and indeed today are robust and resilient. Not only were they responsible for re populating our earth, but they worked long hours in the factories producing clothing and armour for the armies. Some gave birth at their sewing machines.

In yesterday, abortions and adoptions were forced on some due to religious and community traditions. Confusing? On the one hand, their religion would state, "You can't kill an unborn child!" and on the other hand earthlings would say, 'you can't keep a child, you're a single mother, give "it" away." An unborn child now a commodity. Earthlings need to wake up and smell the shit. Deads are evolving faster on earth than earthlings. Why?

The sound of Grunts got louder, Deads are behind me! Screams from a young girl stopped in her tracks, three or four Deads tugging at her. She shouts towards me, "My Baby, save my bab..." "Quick, we can't help her! come on in! Quick! I will get you a fresh bed and a bowl of hot soup." She ran down the few steps, held my arm and pulled me upwards and into the building. I took my last glance at the young girl, now lifeless on the ground. The doors banged closed behind me and the noise of the bolt closing brought me back to reality.

"Follow me; I will take you to your room. Here, I think you will like this room. Take a moment to rest and I will fetch you some hot vegetable soup. Don't be upset, it was to late to save the girl." The door behind me closed, the key turned and locked. It was a small room with a desk, chair, set of drawers and a single bed and another locked door in the corner of the room. Bars on the windows ensured there would be no escape.

My window gave me a view of the young lady in the street. The Deads stood over her, they waited until she rose as a Deads. Screams of a woman from the adjoining room, released me from my gaze towards the street. I tried to get out to help, but my door was locked. "Push! One last push, Push! Fucking well push." This was accompanied by a slap, followed by a whimpering and a long sigh. The room went silent, then a cry from a new baby filled the room.

My door opened with aggression that left a dent in the wall, two men forced a gag into my mouth. Once finished they dragged me along the dirty corridors of the rundown ward, "help me" echoed from each room that I passed. I was Thrown through the doors and landed on the stone floor, as I staggered to my feet the sign above my head read, 'Operating Theatre one.'

As I pulled the bondage from my mouth, the matron greeted me with, "Well dear, are you ready? This won't take long." She turned to the two men. "Strip her." "Keep away from me!" I grabbed a surgical knife from the table and started waving it towards the approaching mens faces. "Now dear, that's not acceptable, put the knife down. We only want to examine you, if you are fit, you will be a mother to one of our millions."

The men stopped in their tracks as I lunged and flicked the scalpel towards their body. "What you mean?"

"Dear, come on, we can't let those Deads take all our children, now, can we? It is our job to re-populate our great country."

"What?" I lunged again with the knife, still managing to keep them at bay

"Think of it as a tree, when one tree is cut down we plant two in its place. I have twin's sperm to fertilise you. Don't you want a child?"

"Fucking look at me! I've had two kids, both are dead. I'm too old..."

She interrupted me, "You are never too old. Your body is fit; you will provide, maybe... two or... four more kids?"

Shaking in pure annoyance, do earthlings never learn? I'm stuck in an abortion clinic, that has now turned to forced conception.

"My body is mine, I make the choices, not you, not my country. Just ME!"

"Look around my dear, do you see anyone willing to help you? Either way you will become pregnant, by force or by choice. Now what will it be?"

The men were jumping backward and forwards as if they were in a boxing match, neither wanting to be sliced. To me, that was a temporary good sign. I was too weak to fight. I continued to sway the blade in the air. If it were not serious, it would have been hilarious to watch our antics.

I pulled my shirt from my trousers and began lifting it, still maintaining my balance and knife swishing. "Good dear, you are coming to your senses..."

"Fuck you! Look," I pulled my shirt higher. "Do you see the scars, I am barren, on the birth of my last child, I took complications, just like my grandmother before me. I no longer can carry a baby and my kids are..."

I fell to the ground exhausted, and sadness overcame me. The men quickly grabbed the knife from my hand and pulled me up onto the table. She pulled my trousers down a little and looked at the scars. "Leave her here, open the closet! she is useless to our cause." She left the room along with one of the men; the other was unlocking the door in the corner. I jumped from the table and stood against the other door to stop anyone getting in or out, it was now one against one.

He walked towards me, then spun on his feet as a Deads pulled at his shoulder. I stood and watched justice rip into his blood covered body, several more Deads entered from the closet.

No sign of anyone in the corridor, I unlocked each door; I was disgusted at what greeted me. Rooms contained pregnant women, some lying on the floor dying, others were pacing the room with madness.

"Stop, how did you get out dear? Quick get her." They ran towards me; theatre one's door opened knocking the man to the ground; a Deads began ravishing on the 'matron.' He squirmed in a circle on the blood that splashed towards him from the matron's jugular. It was the girl in the street, now with more power in her body than she ever had in her earthly existence. She lifted him up by the feet, and sunk her teeth into his groin, ripped it away with one ferocious bite, with what looked like a grin on her face.

I escaped with ten woman and five babies, the others, I couldn't help, but they would soon join the Deads. There was a lorry at the rear of the building full of food and supplies. I drove everyone back to the peaceful fraternity that I left a few hours earlier. Unable to stay, I continued my journey on foot, thinking, I never did get my hot vegetable soup.

Log 9 Jenna

The Year 2016, Folly Beach, South Carolina

    I had spoken to everyone in the 'Folly Beach fraternity,' and the majority decided to leave with me. Others said that they would remain to assist any stragglers and help get them to the safety of the ships.

    After the usual safety briefing, I was feeling rather frisky, and Bret came into my mind. I headed towards his room. His door slightly ajar, he stood leaning against his desk, flicking through some papers with a posture and composure that turned me on.

Bret made me feel at ease; he said all the right words, and I felt comfortable being around him. In the short time I lived at this fraternity, I felt alive, and he treated me like a goddess. It's a physical attraction; I didn't want lovemaking or a relationship. I only required the pleasure that accompanies the function of our inbuilt biological process to reproduce. My over welling desire for Bret to unlock the dirty thoughts filling my brain and to feed my womanly needs, drove me to total distraction. I felt like a sexual creature, and there was no one going to cage me tonight.

The life of a chosen one was mostly
lonely, I entered towns that were desolate,
sometimes not even a DeadS was present.
Loneliness is our unwilling solitude that
earthlings were good at, the DeadS
completed that mission. At night on my
own, in hiding from fear of both
earthlings and DeadS, is not a
comforting place for 'one' to be in.
Morning sunshine brought a slimmer
of comfort and hope. But as your eyes
opened, the reality of the situation kicks
in yet again.

He focused all of his attentions on me, and I'm sure he will continue to do so in a minute or so...

"Bret, are you busy?"

"No, why do you want to talk?"

I am certainly out of practice at being flirtatious but yet I still followed my basic instincts by flickering my eyes, and talking in a lower seductive voice, "I want to do more than talk; I want you to be silent," I closed the door to his room, took the papers from his hand and lay them carefully on the desk. My hormones were running riot, and there was no way I was going to allow anything to kill the mood.

My hands rubbed across his roughly shaved head, he turned me around with his masculine yet gentle touch and lay me on the bed, his lips were soft, our kissing sent shivers and tingles to my heart.

Bret, not that handsome, but I didn't care, he was kind and ever so beautiful from the inside. He had been my loyal friend, since arriving here.

I lay on the bed wiggling and pulling down at my jeans, now I'm in a hurry! Let's dispense with the formalities and romantic gestures, I thought. There was no time for the formal foreplay of touching and kissing for hours on end. It was down to business, and boy was I going to give him a sexual brain freeze! Bret made an attempt at striptease, throwing each garment in a circular motion to the chair at his side while humming a tune. Perhaps this was his way of coming to terms with what was about to occur. He did not have to do any pre-mating ritual, he had me the minute I walked through his door.

Bret laughing and flexing his muscles, he said, "the only pack I have, is hung across the chair along with my clothes." He was a joker, and as far as I was concerned, he didn't need any packs, only the ability to seduce and satisfy.

He was the first. The first since my husband died, and I was damn sure I was going to enjoy every moment. My body craved, and my senses were starved of those enduring earthling pleasures that maintains this earth in existence.

His hand gently caressed my body, but I pulled him closer and tighter, making no mistake that I wanted him, right now. I felt his manhood enter, and he began pulsating inside. I was in the moment, closing my eyes to maximise the sensations, or perhaps just to block the tatty view of the room that we were in.

My back arched upwards as I pushed my head further backward, my hands gripping the sheets and pushing down hard on the bed as my fingers tightened around the sheets. We moved together with a precision and rhythm of a musical overture. He began and continued his thrusting, a couple of minutes later he stopped.

Bret let out a deafening scream!

Fuck, is he finished, I thought?

I screamed at him, "Keep going. Please keep going. I'm nearly there." Arching my back, further backward in my attempt to retain his penetration. As I wriggled from side to side to maximise my pleasure, I felt the swish of liquid between the bed and me. It reminded me of the feeling you get when walking on marshland. I lifted my head forward in acceptance that he had finished. Perhaps the time between sexual encounters had made him end our passion in a frenzy of impatience to arrive at his earthly destination quicker than smashing a Deads brain.

But I was wrong, as I opened my eyes, blood from his severed jugular poured over my body. We were laying in a room full of Deads. They dragged him from my naked blood covered body into the corridor in a mad frenzy of tearing and feeding.

I leaped to my feet pulling at the Deads in an attempt to free Bret, but I was powerless to help and indeed too late. A Deads pushed me to the side, and I slipped on the blood covered floor, awakening several minutes later. I crawled under the bed for safety and to regain my strength amidst the sounds of screaming from the others trapped in the building. My weak body was shivering, I lapsed into a state of unconsciousness.

Awakening to silence, the screaming had gone. I cleaned the blood from my body with Bret's clothes and got dressed. Checking each room for survivors as I navigated down the long dark corridor. I heard a whimpering from a cupboard in the communal kitchen. She was only eight, a little frail child, but she was OK! I pulled her towards me and hugged her tight, to stop her shivering and instill a sense of security. We left the building fast.

There were no others to be saved; we were the only survivors. We talked while we walked, her stories were ghastly. Her young life filled with unimaginable events, Jenna was like a cat with nine lives, only they were running out fast. Each person that had saved her previously were eventually turned by the Deads or abandoned her.

There was something unique about Jenna, but I couldn't fathom it out. Bringing a child into this world and keeping them safe would be an uphill battle for any carer or parent. No Maternity Clinic, no doctor's surgery, no ambulances, no schools, and if lucky a mother or father to keep them safe.

Log 10 Children are the Future

The Year 2016, Wilmington, North Carolina.

Not far to the cruise ships now, we need to sail from New York before the turn to 2017.

After a few days, we arrived at Wilmington. Jenna asked me to take her to the bridge at 'River to the Sea Bikeway.'

"Why, Jenna?"

"My family are there," She said in an eager anticipation.

We arrived tired and hungry, and met a few earthlings near the bridge; they asked what food would I prefer and suggested two excellent restaurants 'The Fish House Grill' or 'The Bridge Tender.' I looked surprised!

"Forgive my humour; those two restaurants used to serve the best seafood and meat in town. All produce locally sourced, and the fish are just jumping to get in."

Only a couple of small fishing boats remained after the Tornado destroyed every other craft. The locals use these for fishing. They found it safer to stay near water; the Deads were smart enough to know that water could trap and kill them.

This area was rich in earthlings, around one thousand lived here, and the largest fraternity that I had come across in my travels.

"We have sent thousands of earthlings to the cruise ships in New York; they are awaiting your arrival. Pleased to meet you, Petre. My name is 'Nav Singhel,' I'm Jenna's grandfather."

He took us to be fed and watered, and afterwards we moved to 'The Waterway Bridge Hotel,' It was now like many other hotels in my travels, a fraternity for the towns remaining earthlings.

I was knackered and fell straight to sleep with Jenna cuddling into me. My dreams were about Willington, known for its ghostly tours and ancient vampire rituals. My dreams consumed my thoughts. We were so close to New York, yet I wondered why the remaining earthlings did not travel with the others.

The crack of thunder made me jump up in haste; Jenna was gone, and so were the others. I staggered to the window; the lightning lit up the sky, and in that brief moment, Jenna and the other remaining earthlings stood on the bridge. Two Deads stood beside them at the end of the bridge.

Everyone knelt down along the edge, Jenna sunk her teeth, first into her grandfather then moved down the line doing the same to the others. I ran from my shelter thinking Jenna was in trouble,

"Leave her alone; Please Leave her, I beg you."

At first, I thought I had failed her. Another fierce flash of lightning this time hitting the water below the bridge. The water now red from the blood that spilled from their necks. I stood on the bridge a few feet from Jenna and held out my arms for her to come to me.

"I owe my life to you Petre. After earthlings

murdered my mother and father, I became the last remaining vampire. These are now my followers."

She raised her hands towards the sky, and everyone rose from their knees on the bridge, each holding hands, they had now joined the realm of the vampires.

"Petre, we are from the same bloodline, I'm a rebel, my parents and I escaped the realms of the vampires just before the vampires joined and evolved with the vamptures. The vamptures murdered my parents because they refused to evolve with them."

She held her hands further towards the skies; I wanted a final hug from this unique child.

A rift appeared in the sky above, each one drifted upwards including the two Deads. They vanished into the crack of the realm; Jenna looked at me with love and compassion. In that brief moment we exchanged our thoughts, she would indeed return to help save the Earthlings.

Children are the future of our earth.

Log 11 Spy Hotel

The Year 2016, Morehead, North Carolina

Five hundred and eight miles now separate New York and me. American now overrun with Deads, I need to get all the cruise ship earthlings to the safety of Europe and find the cure.

Another day in my journey, nightfall and I still needed to find a safe place. As I approached the edge of the forest, a pathway became visible. At first, I hesitated and then went for it, I ran through the wood, the trees blocked out the moon. I arrived at the entrance. The sign overhead was lit up with a neon light, 'The Morehead City Tonhil hotel, North Carolina.'

Another sign next to the gates surrounded by a high fence perimeter stated. 'If you can read this sign, you are welcome,' underneath there was a button it read 'push for admittance.' The front gates opened, I stepped forward five feet, the gates behind me closed, then the next set of gates opened. I repeated this ritual three times in total, before walking down the driveway towards the front entrance that was lit up like Christmas.

Actually, we are only two weeks away from Christmas. Traditions now had little meaning. Fraternities contained earthlings from many denominations and faiths; it was impossible to cater for each one. And in the interest of their safety, patrolling the grounds became their worship. Some still took a personal moment to pray for their faith.
Even when a herd of Deads were killed, the will to cheer was replaced by a sadness of 'That could have been someone close to them.

The first set of gates were secure, but the others did need a little repair. I had the feeling that someone was watching me. As I arrived at the door, I was greeted by a man dressed as a butler, while a butch lady shone a torch into my eyes.

"She looks Fit."

I was ushered into a brightly lit room and told to strip naked. The examination was carried out by two husky built women looking for cuts, bruises or infected wounds.

"You can't be too careful." She turned towards the other lady and shouted. "ALL CLEAR"

New clothes were thrown at my feet. "Get dressed, and you can meet our general manager," I felt uncomfortable as I bent down, and dressed in front of their glares.

I was led to a lavish room, filled with antiques, paintings, and books. Unbelievable that such places still exist.

"I'm Reikan, welcome to my hotel, You can check out at any time, But you can never leave."

She stood up from her leather armchair and laughed while stretching out her hand. She had a firm handshake and made sure I knew who the boss was.

Reikan had a smirk on her face as she spoke: "of course you can leave, I just get a kick out of saying that. We don't need to force our guest to stay." She walked around, and sat on the corner of her luxurious oak desk, looked me straight in the eyes, while trying to suss me out.

"We charge 100 dollars per night, follow me."

I received a guided tour of the hotel and its

grounds. At the rear of the hotel, there was an area behind a line of fruit trees; I was told to keep out! This is the only sector that's out of bounds. Vegetables in abundance were grown in plots dotted around the grounds. This fraternity is nearly self-sufficient.

"As a guest, you will be required to pay your one hundred dollars by doing work. You will be handsomely paid! You have a choice of Housekeeping, Kitchen, Security, Repairs, Food Hunter, Equipment hunter or my favourite, a Precious Hunter; that's searching out antiques and goods worthy of my protection." She stopped to take a breath after her rehearsed speech

I thought she was joking about the room charge!

"No rush, give me your answer in the morning. Get some sleep; you will have an early rise."

"I don't need to wait till morning, I love hunting, I will help you hunt for food."

"Agreed."

She left, I remained for a few minutes', and looked upwards towards the full moon, lovely and bright. Like a hot bath, for those brief moment's, all worries and concerns disappeared. In the peacefulness, my mind drifted, "let's go kids." A tear dropped to the ground, as I returned to this reality.

Each room in the hotel could hold two to four earthlings in comfort. There were 220 rooms, and she ran a professional hotel operation. Doubt the original owners would be returning for their share of the profits.

I decided not to inform anyone here of my real identity, not yet, or at least until I fully understood this place. Experience has taught me that not everything looks as good as what it is.

The hotel had guards that paraded the outside and inside perimeters with military precision. This is certainly a hotel that Deads or unruly earthlings would not want to mess with.
My fellow guests are happy, and they feel safe living here. No one talks about leaving. I've been here a week and still don't feel comfortable, so I have decided that it would be a bad idea, to ask anyone to leave and join me.

I approached the GM's office to inform her that I would be continuing my journey tomorrow.

[Five hundred and eighty-one miles separated me from New York's Cruise Ships. It was time to leave; It has taken almost sixteen years to get this far. Now I was impatient; I needed to make the final push to the ships before new years eve, leaving me seven days to get there. My connection with my allies has informed me that the ships will come under attack in the harbours, to curtail the vast numbers trying to make passage to other countries. The ships need to depart on new year's day, at the latest.]

The door to her office was open, I walked in to find another concealed door slightly ajar, inquisitive, I went in for a look.

The room was filled with CCTV screens that captured every room, nook, and cranny of the hotel. It covered the grounds, including the forbidden area. I stood and watched in horror for a few minutes.

Back trotting, I quietly exited her office, stood at the door and knocked as loud as I could, shouting, "HELLO Mam, are you there?"

"WAIT THERE; I will be out in a second."

I don't think anyone is allowed to leave, after all; thankfully I am a food hunter. I won't be telling her of my intentions.

"What can I do for you Petre?" said, as she tucked in her low cut red blouse into her black mini skirt. She turned around and looked back into the room.

"That will be all Bloomer. You can finish off that report tomorrow."

Bloomer, as she was known, was a highly attractive woman, she dressed well, and always had a smile for the ladies. I overheard one of the young male guards mutter, "she is wasted," now I know what he meant, but not a waste for our GM.

"Well, what can I do for you?" from the frustration in her voice, I could feel that I interrupted her at the wrong moment.

"Will it be OK with you if I attend the afternoon food hunt? I'm feeling a bit under the weather, and would love that extra rest in the morning," she looked at me as if I had grown a set of horns,

"I suppose so," the door slammed in my face.

I took a deep breath and returned downstairs, to ponder what I had just viewed on those hidden screens. I lay in bed, and could not decide what to do or whom to trust. No one person stood out; quite a few guests were related, aunts, uncles, niece's and nephews of the GM. They were intricated into the fabric of this hotel, in an attempt to protect their new family asset.

The GM had another working group, one she did not mention, a private group, unknown to the guests; they were Deads hunters.

Deads were kept alive in this fraternity. The elderly, infirm and any new guest who can't offer any contribution are fed to those Deads. And the Deads are being fed to the hotel guests.

In my short stay, thankfully I never eat any meat. I often wondered, how meat was served on a daily basis to the guest? As a food hunter, not once did we bring home meat.

What they were doing was horrific and scandalous, but I had to leave tomorrow, no time to bring this to light and indeed would they care? As I lay in my bed, I was approached by a young, frail couple,

"You have seen the cameras? take us with you. We will be next to die."

[Unknown to the GM, the meat from the Deads torso slowly destroys the earthling's antibodies, and are responsible for an internal virus that attacks their mesentery organ. Their digestive system in disarray, they become weak and eventually die.]

"Be ready for the afternoon food hunt, we will leave then, let's meet at the garden next to the gates."

The lady whispered into my ear,

"If we don't meet you, head to the theme park, it's ten miles north from here. "Charles will be waiting for you."

She kissed me on the cheek, and as she was leaving the room, she said, "Sleep well. Our Chosen One."

I slept through the night and did not awake until it was time to move. I searched for the couple, but they had disappeared. As I was leaving the gates, the GM approached me.

" Helga and Jo, why were they in your room last night?"

I turned and watched my hunting group enter the first gate, as I stepped forward, she grabbed my arm; I turned to face her

"They asked me to find some canned fruit, I better catch up with the group," I pointed towards the forest, "don't want to be out there on my own."

She let my arm go, I turned and walked forward into the first gate, when the doors closed; I shouted out

"Do you know where they are? They were to meet me here and say what fruit they wanted."

"Get any fruit," and she walked away.

The final gate opened and as we made our exit, a group of Deads took everyone by surprise. While the Deads consumed my group, other Deads had managed to get through the gate system. As I escaped into the forest, I heard the GM scream

"Secure the gates, secure..."

Deads attacked her from behind; they were no longer her captors.

Log 12 Up Up and Away

The Year 2016, Outskirts of Morehead, North Carolina.

Running until my body said stop! A few more miles until I reach the theme park. How did they know! What is at the Theme Park? Who is Charles? Too many questions, needing answers.

Not a sound as I reached the park, not a person in sight. Don't know why, but I was expecting a theme park full of earthlings, all screaming with excitement having fun and laughter.

That's the way it used to be, apart from the occasional mugger, or shooter who took the lives of innocent children, because they had a fight with their teacher, or just because! Just because it was easy to carry a gun, and despite leaders promising to reduce gun crime, each one failed to perform on their election promises. Just like our 1984 meeting, leaders were good at promising the earth but delivering lies and deceit instead.

"Petre, Petre, over here, I'm Charles, follow me."
I certainly heard those words before, and it sure didn't go down well. Still, I liked his voice and followed him; we ran, not upright, but crouched down, hugging the boundary of the rides, hiding from someone.

"Look, look upwards."

"Wow, what's that?" In the near distance a colourful display, half a rainbow moon, protruding from the rooftops of some buildings.

"Stop! Some Deads are wandering in front of my hot air balloon.

"You're what?"

"Hot air balloon! Hi, my name is Charles Green."

"Charles Green, WOW you have not aged one bit, you are nearly two hundred and thirty years old."

"They're gone. RUN. Petre, come on run faster."

Charles was busy getting us safely away. I lay on the floor of the balloon looking towards the sky as it turned to night. The blasts of fire lighting up the sky with a beautiful glow. Safe at last, I don't think Deads can fly, well not yet anyway.

Charles held out his hand and pulled me to my feet. The ground getting smaller as we rose into the night sky, it was a clear night, and the stars were out in force.

"That's the north star" he pointed

"Polaris and there is the Big Dipper" I pointed

"You know your stars, Petre."

We both hugged and laughed.

"You're safe now; I have enough food and fuel to get you to New York without landing."

"How? "This size balloon would consume around

20 gallons of propane per hour, would it not?"

Charles held up a small pea-sized pellet.

"This is the new fuel; I designed the product to save the planet from greenhouse emissions, and cheap fuel for earthlings. The fuel companies along with the military stole my designs and silenced me."

He showed me a box, full of pellets.

"These are the last ones, enough for me to get you to your ship and to make a few other journeys to save more earthlings."

We wrapped a blanket around us and cuddled to keep warm in the crisp cold night.

"I am a descendant from Charles Green, born in 1785 in Britain."

I asked Charles, "Was he the one that pioneered the use of gas, from coal in place of hydrogen?"

"Yes, Inventing has been in our family since then, my father and his father developed different types of fuel. It will take us around thirty hours to get to New York, providing the winds don't turn against us."

We talked and talked until we both fell asleep. My

eyes opened to the sounds of grunts, my body trained to differentiate between earthling and Deads.

Charles was bitten, a Deads was chewing on his torso. Three other Deads slid down from the top of the balloon, their fingers ripping into the Dacron as they fell into the basket. The basket began filling with blood, I tried to clamber out of the balloon, but they pulled me back in. I slipped and fell; my head now submerged in the basket full of blood.

"Petre, Petre, stop, calm down...Petre, It's Charles, your OK. Please sit down."

Charles held and hugged me tight. "I thought I had lost you; you were screaming, crying and shouting, then you tried to jump out of the basket."

"I'm sorry Charles, I'm sorry."

We then had a great conversation, some wine, and cheese, high in the sky and free from fear, apart from my nightmares. When you have witnessed what I have, those will always return, whenever I feel safe.

Charles pointed to the distance, "There is your ship. "Berthed at the Manhattan Cruise Terminal."

It was majestic; my ship was the Queen Mary. My husband and I spent a romantic time on that ship. At one time it was berthed as a hotel in Long Beach. He gave me my first driving lesson in the car-park next to where it was berthed. I told him that the ship is haunted, "that's great," he said, "we can ask for a discount if we have to share a room with a ghost!" Fond memories, memories that keep the horrors at bay.

First stop Ireland, then she would sail to the River Clyde, to shores where she was built in 1936. It was an old ship, but could carry three thousand two hundred and forty souls, including crew. In 1942, she took sixteen thousand and eighty-two American soldiers to Britain to help in the second world war.

There were around three hundred ships berthed; I was hoping to save over a million earthlings and bring them to safety. I had made it to New York at last. Leaving my homeland would be sad. But I needed to find the cure, to stop this frenzy and heal the cracks in the realms, before earthlings became extinct.

Log 13 Europe is Falling China is Building

The Year 2016, New York harbor

    I arrived to a cheering crowd, and now I will lead my followers to the kingdom of salvation - Europe. Finally, my journey begins, the last sixteen years have not been in vain, I have managed to save over one million earthlings, earthanity now stands a chance of survival.

    Three hundred ships have set sail; ten ships will remain for another week. Every earthling understands that we are heading towards countries, that have a fear and armies that will kill. However, I have been promised safe passage for my ships.

The Year 2016, December 26th, North Atlantic Ocean.

Two days into our sailing and the passengers on the ships are terrified at the news broadcast received from our allies: 'Croatia, Romania, and Serbia are now fighting creatures from another realm. Dead earthlings who are buried with a stake in their heart rose from their graves and are feeding on their living communities.'

[This remains a modern local tradition, despite being banned by the immersion into Europe in the 1990's. When earthlings report seeing a visual image of a deceased, they dig up the body from the grave and hammer a wooden stake into the lifeless hearts. Some families' drove them into the heart before burial]

China once held the worst human rights record; now the European militia has won and taken over the award outright. The only Chinese earthlings sacrificed, are those who died while rebuilding and extending the Great Wall around cities. Chinese are still helping earthlings from different countries, and are the only producers of the needed rubber. They barter for some other supplies and earthanity reasons. Millions of other earthlings are flooding in to help continue the construction.

The first containment centre is constructed adjoining the Jiumenkou wall near the Shanhaiguan Pass, know as, "great pass over water." Over the centuries these locations became a strategic position, and many battles took place. The dead went to 'the Guan's Realm.' Chinese believe they will return and protect earthlings from the other realms.

While Deads do not like water, they will find a way around. The stories of floaters surviving in the seas are untrue. They will die if submerged in water for a lengthy period and sea creatures will feast on the Deads decaying bodies.

In the Chinese chambers, earthlings live in the first layer for three days and move to the second for another three days. In total ten containment layers are traversed before they are allowed access to the protected city.

So far China is free from all realms and is the safest place to be. We have one hundred ships sailing towards China. Fifty ships towards Derry and one hundred and fifty to other parts of Europe.

The Chinese are manufacturing ancient herbal remedies, known for keeping the vampire realm at bay, or so ancient history dictates. They are working every second to try and reproduce these treatments. How good the potion will fair against Vamptures is unknown

The European militia, instead of cremation for the millions of butchered earthling's corpses, dumped the bodies in heaps, on the island of Jersey and Guernsey. The stench from bodies reached the realm of the vampires. This is no ordinary vampire, but a vulture type, known as a 'Vampture.'

Darwin described vultures as disgusting and unearthly creatures. However, in reality, they played a significant cleansing role throughout the world until earthlings took them to extinction.

Vultures and vampires evolved and created a new species and their realm changed. Some vampires resisted the change and are in hiding, like Jenna, but the majority adapted, and now they are part of the new realm. The scent of decay awoke the Vamptures, who are now flying to feed on the earthling's decaying carcasses, devouring any earthling they encounter on their travels.

This evil will avoid a disease ridden epidemic for earthlings. Worse still, now Vamptures will compete with Deads when they finish cleansing the corpses. Its a race or a fight, who will get to the earthlings first, Deads or the Vamptures?

My birthright in saving humanity is becoming nearly impossible; I shall rise to my task as the Divine

God's requested, their faith in me will not go unrewarded.

Log 14 Heads of the Deads

Recapping of past lost Logs in the year 2000 to 2016

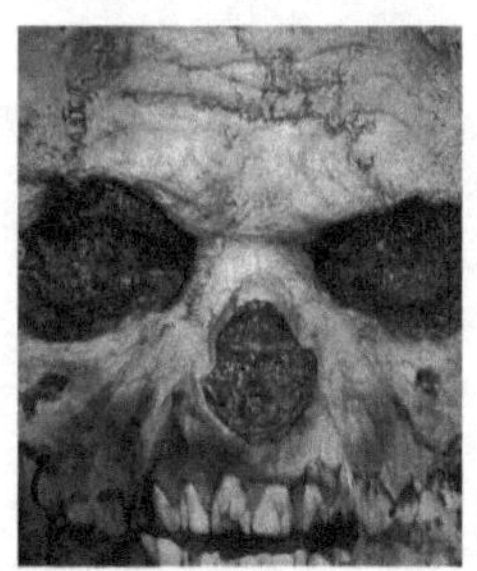

I studied Deads for sixteen years and is remarkable how they do not deteriorate at all. Body gashes, open flesh wounds and cracked exposed bones do not rot or decay any further after their turning. They achieve their eternal beauty and do not age; earthlings would pay a high price for this longevity drug.

Insects, flies, bees and other flying entity do not invade Deads bodies but hover away from them.

Deads do not possess any foul odour like a conventional decaying corpse, though the sight of one makes the living heave with sickness. Unable to live in water, they can stand in the rain for months or years, but they cannot be submerged, or decay will begin. The water turns them into sustainable and safe food for the sea creatures.

The methods of killing a Deads is to destroy their brain or submerge in liquid for several hours. Limbs severed will regrow. Their heads can live without a body provided contact with blood every few days is established. Studies are being carried out with their brains. Stored within glass chambers these, in turn, are wired with many supercomputers, creating a unit with a supremely high level of computational capacity. The only two countries able to provide such power and technology is China and Russia.

The European militia send hunters to American soil to bring Deads heads back for testing. In these visits, not once did they offer any form of help or medicines for earthlings. They wrote every earthling in the Americas off.

Countries bordering Russia claimed leadership and destroyed all research that they had pioneered and collected.

Russians now doomed by their fellow earthlings, and their nearby allies turned the country into what the West calls " a Third world." Despite China sending assistance, internal conflicts still exist in Russia. We are not aware yet if China managed to secure the brain research technology.

Log 15 Deads are far from Dead

Recapping of past lost Logs in the year 2000 to 2016

My mind drifts and I find myself reliving old memories I witnessed in the past. These memories will help us understand the forces we are dealing with.

I was chased by some Deads and entered an old dark warehouse; it smelt of foul and stagnant water. Grunts from Deads got closer, I entered the first room and locked the door. The room contained a broken desk, papers lay scattered on the floor, it was a small room with space to hold a few earthlings. A surveillance window pointed towards the factory floor.

Owners would keep an eye on their forced labour, refugees from the conflicts in the 'Middle East,' they would work and sleep on the floors next to their machinery.

This factory was overlooked by the authorities, the military needed garments produced at any earthling cost to protect soldiers from the bites. Little that did them! Everyone in the warehouse, workers and owners, now joined as one and working together in harmony, as Deads.

I was confined in that room for seven days without food or clean water. Condensation dripped from the glass above my head and kept me hydrated. As the days rolled by, I became delusional and now after years of reflection, what I witnessed proved to be the beginning of evolution from Deads on earth.

Two-way glass allowed me to observe their daily rituals. A Deads threw another against my window, I jumped backward, startled with fright, but managed to keep silent. The thump on the window began their passion. Two Deads became intertwined in the emotions of what the earthling would call a 'hot and passionate love making ritual for one overcome with desire for each other.'

At first, this scene made me feel, sick to my stomach, Deads in an embrace. But I recalled what the divine gods told me, 'all forms from the realms do procreate, within their realm.' Deads do in fact live. Who was I to be presumptuous, believing earthlings, are the only ones that partake in stimulating, and exciting acts beyond the basic need of reproduction.

Too painful to contemplate Deads doing what earthlings have done since their existence on earth. These thought processes come from our dictated upbringing in society, and our parents, and their parents and so forth. Earthlings are shaped and molded into the society to which they belong; this is a form of forced and dictated evolution. Hence, why battles and confrontation exist between different cultures, and within individual beliefs.

After the rituals between the Deads had passed, a stray earthling entered the warehouse. She walked towards me and stood next to the window; I saw sadness and bewilderment, yet she appeared to be looking for something.

I was unable to bang on the window to warn her, without the fear of alerting the other Deads, I looked into this young woman's eyes. Alone and desolate, her clothes torn and dirty.

For the brief time, our eyes joined, I saw, heard and felt the pain of what she endured over the last few days. Her children and family decimated by Deads. In my visions, she held her baby in her arms while the remainder of her family turned. She ran from the turning Deads, and fell, the baby tumbled, rolling into the fast flowing river, lost forever.

Our eye contact ceased as a distraught wolf came in, and leaped towards her arm, dragging her to the ground, she only screamed once. The sound alerted the Deads, they ignored the woman and ravished on the wolf consuming the entire animal including the bones. When finished a smear of blood became the only trail of the wolf's existence.

The young woman staggered to her feet, and walked out of the warehouse, none of the Deads pursued her. My first thought, she is immune and I, at last, found a cure. I took my chance and escaped my confinement; I caught up with her. My hand touched her shoulder, and I saw what she saw, the process of turning consumed her body.

This encounter led me to an idea and a concept of protection; I explained this to our leader, she dismissed my idea, and I departed the fraternity for my safety. Arriving at another new fraternity, the earthlings within it unsure and with no real leader to keep them safe. They listened to me; I did not want to be their leader, but together we could all be safe. We captured one Deads, and each member including any new stray earthling looking to join was made to walk passed the caged creature.

I discovered when an earthling is infected; Deads make a low-key pitched but eerie noise. When a non-infected earthling passes a Deads, their voice becomes more intense, higher pitched and a sound to chill you to the bone. Insisting no harm to the captured Deads, we continued and only kept one in the cage for one week, released and a new fresh Deads captured.

Years passed quick, and I visited many more states to try and get as many earthlings to the Cruise Ships as possible. Regular, ship radio broadcasts, let all passengers know of my research and they await my arrival. They want a cure and an end to the turnings. Their protection lay in Europe, and once more they would walk free, without fear or intimidation with their remaining friends and family.

I formed a strong alliance with one of our European allies. I communicate my knowledge as I speak from within my soul, all communications are sent by a form of ancient mediated telepathic signals, via the Divine gods. I do not know whom this person is. But I feel a lost and secure connection; they dissipate the information to our allies.

They want my assistance and research; it's a matter of time before Deads reach Europe. They know the world could be overrun with Deads, and earthlings will be in the minority, perhaps become extinct.

My European allies believe I am the chosen one to find the cure. Some sceptics say these Deads are hell's damnation.

They are not a work of what earthlings call "hell," they are a calling from the realms of the gods. Perhaps to purify this earth, to make the necessary changes to stop the world at each other's throats, with war's, spiritual battles, land space or wanting to be the dominant earthling force.

Should fate befall me, my writings and research need to be given to the next in line.

Log 16 Zombie or DeadS

Recapping of History Log's

I did say the word Zombie does not feature in my writings. However, my European allies should consider the following. The DeadS who walk on earth are sometimes referred to as a Zombie by the masses of earthlings. The name 'ZOMBIE' was first recorded in 1819 in England. However, the DeadS existed as far back as the year 1,000 BC.

It is believed throughout the world that Zombies

materialised as reincarnated flesh eaters, via magic. Research, if taken in the context of modern day films and stories, will point you to the untruth.

France, Brazil, Haitian and West Africa mentioned the term Zombie in their historical writings. Do not be mistaken this is not folklore. This is valid evidence, misinterpreted and listed as fictional folklore and termed 'Zombie.'

Zombies are created by magic, radiation and mental disease, are misleading claims by our government officials. Voodoo cults in Haiti and European folklore called Zombies "the undead." Popular culture believes this unnatural death came from aliens or outer space.

The elders of earthanity witnessed films portraying zombie-like creatures; these films are thought to originate from folklore. These writers are represented as visionaries of fictional creativity. Some Earthlings accused and slaughtered them for bringing on the wrath of the gods through their obsession with horror films.

The truth of zombies were hidden and justified in public as folklore by governments in an attempt to cover up those infected. The authorities did, as usual, extraordinarily well in "pulling the wool" over the eyes of their earthlings. When earthlings started acting strange but did not show the full flesh eating zombie disorders, psychologists stepped in by order of the government.

These doctors gave names to such individuals as having a mental illness or schizophrenia. Governments lied to their followers, instead of finding answers for a cure, they allowed the film industry and the medical profession to make false claims. By releasing artistic images representing some of the earthlings found in our society. Earthlings became obsessed by prejudices, and they turned on each other.

Throughout time earthlings turned a blind eye to Deads. Stories and films of zombies made the truth disappear. Now Deads are back, earthlings throughout the world at first turned to their religious leaders for hope and salvation. These same leaders continued to pursue their unhealthy deeds on their fellow earthlings.

Revisit folklore information and take what you can. Any cure will be held deep in the mystical writings. You will not find solutions in any zombie film. In 1864 the Haitians passed a law crediting the term of 'zombie' as official.

A book written by W C Seebrook in 1929, "The Magic Island," it holds a hidden piece of vital information. Seek out the writings of the Hieronymite monk Ramón Pané in the year 1493, unknown to him it contains secret words. These books and the European heritage will be invaluable.

Log 17 Sickness and Panic

The Year 2016, December 30th, North Atlantic Ocean.

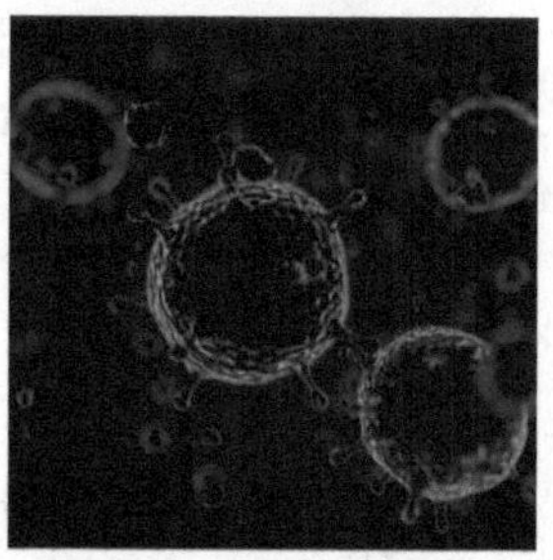

Five days at sea and sickness rules our vessel. The ships drastic and violent movements in the squall of the waves killed forty earthlings, their bodies crushed by moving furniture. Any fixtures not screwed down are tossed overboard.

The bug befalling the passengers is a new strain never witnessed before, at first, we blamed the extreme turbulent weather. But soon discovered that it was a strain from a Deads, we are keeping this news a secret until we are sure of what is occurring.

Earthlings are being urged to stay in their cabins and only attend the doctor on an emergency. Fear is starting to increase, a craft full of healthy earthlings now spiralling downhill. We remained free from infection for many years. I do not understand why and what is happening.

Despite our best efforts, we are unable to come up with an answer on the origination or how the disease is being transmitted. Pathogens that originated from a Deads have been discovered, yet not one person has been bitten.

Before a body turns, they are thrown overboard and become fodder for the sea. I asked the captain to keep one for examination, but he overruled me. Regardless of the captain's orders, we secured a few corpses. Serious problems will exist in Europe and indeed the Earth if the virus is airborne. Ireland is five more days away; we need answers sooner than later. If the virus is airborne, then the ship and its passengers will need to be set ablaze before we reach shore.

Earthlings are refusing to eat or drink, and are becoming lifeless. Panic replaced with a dread of death and returning as Deads. Those who listened to my stories are not afraid, but they are confused. If they do return as Deads, will they be murdered yet again?

Like a priest sitting by the dying earthling, all I can offer is the knowledge that the transference to another state of existence will occur. This will be no different from the turbulent, yet beautiful first birth when arriving from the loins of their mothers. Covered with a little blood and for some, screaming their way out of the birthing channel.

The transformation from earthling to Deads will be the same as their first delivery to this world. Again they will crave on their creation, the nurturing milk of their turned life. This will be the blood of others. Cravings to feed and turn other earthlings into Deads will be so overwhelming that family choice would make no difference to their choice of nourishment. The Deads are so overwhelmed with the need to feast and repopulate their own.

Log 18 This is my Sadness and Pain

The Year 2016, December 30th, North Atlantic Ocean. Recapping memories.

When you are born, you will die. And when you die, you will live, do not be afraid to die. Earthlings can vary with different degrees towards good and evil. Likewise, the other realms possess similar abilities.

After I had diagnosed my mother's illness, many earthlings invaded our home looking for answers to their conditions, my nightmares and threats towards my family became a regular occurrence. Dad sent me to relatives in China, and I learnt their rituals of meditation.

On my return as an adult, we relocated to New Orleans, to protect my family and the powers I possessed. The town was rich in voodoo and witchcraft; I blended in. This city full of passion and delight, is where I met my husband, and we married without any fuss, only a few attended. Both of his parents were dead; he is the son of Michael, our Irish friends. Both shared the same name, an old tradition, to name your first born boy after your own name. Our union received a blessing, with the birth of two children a boy and a girl.

My parents, both knowing what is about to occur on earth, committed suicide at the stroke of midnight on 31st December 1999. Their note, "you are the chosen one, the realm of the Souls need us, we are so sorry we cannot stay, love you, mum and dad. Kiss, kiss."

My twins and husband were murdered during the first week of the American cataclysm while trying to return home to America. Prejudices and hatred towards Americans and the fear of contamination took my babies. They had just turned sixteen.

Londoners killed everyone on their school trip, kids, parents, and teachers. I insisted their dad went with them as an assistant to help; I could not bear the thought of them being alone, without Michael or me. News channels around the world filled the televisions with graphic images of earthlings turning and rampaging, Deads tearing and consuming everyone in their path.

Europeans started their massacre, beginning with anyone from the Americas, next turning on their fellow earthlings.

My entire family dead. At first, I contemplated my death, but the ancient meditation rituals blocked me from this pathway. My work as the chosen one continued. I couldn't let their deaths perish on earth in vain.

Grief will now be part of my natural fabric and shape me. No longer to be the person I used to be. As I reawaken, I refuse to allow my pain to be misguided, confused or muddled. Accepting the present, and working to relive my past with their thoughts, the happiness and sadness we all shared. They are now gone, but we will meet again in the realm of the souls, perhaps for eternity or a just a fleeting moment.

Reinvesting my energy into helping all earthlings, who want or need my help. Love and wisdom are my companionships, this is the real strength of the righteous earthling, and will be paramount in the rebuilding of our grief and community.

Every earthling has experienced loss and betrayal from the Gods, or is it betrayal from Earthlings themselves? Yet, it is taken on the chin, as a 'plan' from creation.

My loss is my Sadness and Pain.

Log 19 The Mosquito

The Year 2016, December 30th, North Atlantic Ocean.

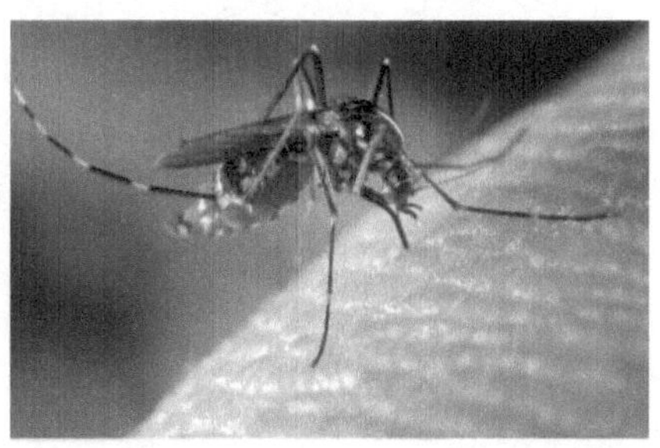

    We discovered the outbreak is not airborne. The bite mark found on the autopsy is so small to be a human bite; we are carrying out further investigation to uncover their origin. We informed the captain of our findings.

    Concerned for the baby growing inside her womb, one of the young prostitutes came for examination, her baby due any time. She lay on a battered and worn out medical bed, waiting for a nurse to attend. Time slowed to a fraction of reality. In slow motion, I witnessed something incredible.

A mosquito made a direct flightpath towards her as if it was destined to do so. The mosquito landed on her neck, the same location as the other examined bodies. Neither nurse or patient noticed the Mosquito, I did.

The scene, reminiscence of holding negatives of a film up towards the light, and moving them one frame at a time. As the nurse continued her prodding, the wings carried the tiny and insignificant body closer. Size on earth towards spreading disease holds no significance. She was close to giving birth, it landed and gnawed at her neck before flying away.

The insect made no attempt to escape as I captured it in a glass container. The woman left the room with a clean bill of health from the nurse.

"Marvin, I need your assistance," I took my colleague into a private room, and explained that I needed his skills to dissect and confirm my initial thoughts.

He pushed his broken glasses above his head, "how? Your research proves this is not possible. Flies and mosquito's lived on the ship for years without any incident, Why now?" Putting his glasses on his eyes, he sat down with his hands to his head and moaned in bewilderment.

Despite our disbelieve, Marvin discovered that the mosquito did carry the new strain of Deads within its DNA. He declared, "This broke new grounds, while the virus is not airborne, it is with the Mosquito."

Everyone became mystified? Mosquito's don't go near Deads, and insects cannot become infected.

My research now under scrutiny, and unable to connect with my dreams to access the knowledge of the Divine Gods, I became lost for answers. This new direction changed the game plan.

Earthlings would not sleep, each movement or skin crawl felt like a Mosquito. Hysteria took hold and the captain ordered the entire ship to be searched, every corner and crevice to be investigated. Fighting mosquito's became an almost impossible battle to win.

The Mosquito blood contained a RAT's DNA.

[The word, R. A. T, is spelt out and not said, this is a superstition of seafarers and of the nomadic country of the Manx where they are called long-tails. I advise our European allies to do likewise.]

Our ship's captain stunk with the scent of pipe

smoke, he was a tall and skinny man, and always dressed in his tattered cruise line uniform. He upheld his rank at all times. His father named him Vitus, after the famous Danish navigator who served in the Russian navy.

Vitus announced, they found a Deads corpse in the bottom of the ship, with long-tail bite marks.

Stocker was responsible for keeping a fire burning in the depths of the hull. He kept his wife tied in chains. Her body lay on the ground; her head smashed beyond recognition. Stocker, sat crying "what have I done to everyone on this ship?"

Dead, R. A. T. S, lay close to the body; another long-tail attempted to feast from the Deads, on its first bite it died. This confirmed no other breathing creature apart from the wolf, holds the virus and turns.

What about the mosquito? For Analysis we caught over one hundred other mosquito's, not one contained the pathogen. We witnessed a freak occurrence of a Mosquito and long tail mutating. 'A one in a trillion chance.'

This proves when an earthling has turned to Deads, and when that Deads die, their virus passing abilities die at the same time as they die. Thus, making contamination impossible for any insect or animal to occur from eating Deads.

The passengers and crew are now more content; we are only one day away from shore and have managed to contain the epidemic.

Log 20 The Cure

The Year 2016, December 31st, Ten miles from the Port of Derry, Ireland.

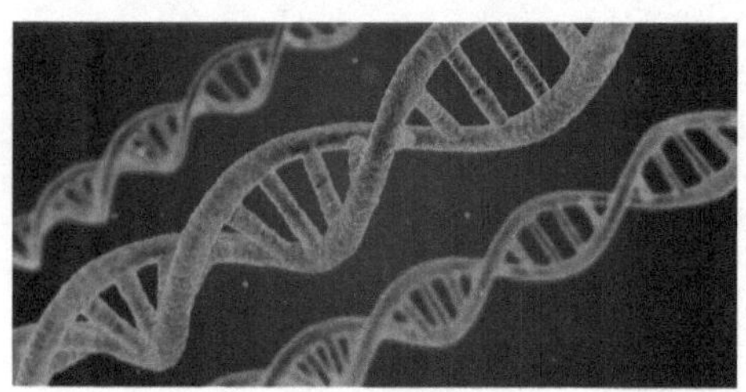

Full of self-doubt, I believe, and then I don't. How can I be the chosen one? Perhaps my Irish allies are to continue my research and find a cure. The shore of Ireland now a few hours away. The ship is overrun with Deads and only a few earthlings remain.

The mosquito infected more earthlings than what we realised, and the curfew kept passengers away from the surgery. They turned to Deads in the comfort of their cabins.

The young prostitute staggered through the corridor, blood dripping from her mouth as she fed on a child held tight in her arms. Discarded to the floor, the boy rose to his feet and began a frenzy of cruel, violent torture on another unlucky passenger. I turned and awaited my fate, a loud scream from behind made me turn around. With no fight left in her frail body, the once beautiful nurse became their next victim. Unable to help I ran to my cabin.

If I turn or die, find religious leaders with a genuine faith of others. These leaders must be unafraid and love Deads as their own. The only way to communicate with realms is with a full understanding of the rights of the Divine Gods and the different divisions of our place on earth and of the other realms.

Seek my next in blood line, and with the others, they are the real salvation of earthlings on this earth. The vastness of the European culture and the roots in our Celtic countries hold the answers to our quests to save earthlings.

In a fear to be called insane, I held back one piece of vital evidence; I need to tell you now. The Deads last ran free in the year 1,000 BC. They came to cleanse our earth from the earthling created evils. The cure came from my ancestors with the assistance of the faiths.

Some Deads remained here while respecting each other's rights. As you are aware we live in a world so complex and full of atrocities, Deads gained stronger powers allowing their return.

This story told to me by a dying earthling, in my arms as he turned. Grunts and gnawing sounds blended to make sense; I understood every word the Deads spoke.

He outlined the historical values of European culture and my destiny to lead earthlings to Europe. This is the only time I communicated with a Deads.

Historical Traditions are contained in the water and the passing of water, this plays an important part in the earthling's salvation. Search out these places, and the waters it contains. You will need the power of the wise leaders and a bloodline of a chosen one. Put your faith in those stepping forward and show both courage and freedom for the earthlings of our dying world.

When the ship berths, there is no doubt Ireland will be thrown into the darkness of time. My allies must embrace this challenge with all their soul. The Deads will rampage through your countryside and cities, turning as many as they can while they run on their hunger killing spree. The earthlings are their food for survival, and for those that perish they to will become the sole mates of the Deads.

Log 21 Port of Derry

The Year 2016, December 31st, Time 23.45 Port of Derry.

The ship crashed into the port of Derry destroying the harbour to a pile of rubble. Deads disembarked in their thousands, 'may the divine gods be with our Irish allies.' They will want to feed and turn others.

Are Deads to rule earth and have access to the

realms of the souls?

England, Scotland, and Wales have other problems with impending Vampure attacks from Europe. So much so, England recalled their militia back from Ireland. Now Ireland is on their own, and facing the wrath of the disembarking Deads.

I'm still an earthling, and on Irish soil, my destiny is to find the cure and send the Deads back to their realms, this I cannot do on my own. I need to locate my allies, and we will defend the earthlings.

As I left my cabin and proceeded to walk up the stairway to the open deck, an eerie silence grabbed my soul. My hand reached to turn the handle and escape the confines of the vessel.

Bone chilling screams stopped me in my tracks, and instead of running, I turned around and walked down the stairs towards the room where the screams originated. More screams, manlier, and not from the same person.

I reached for the door, another scream, I wanted to run, but I couldn't. I peeked into the room, a man lay on the ground, his legs chewed and severed from his body; he couldn't move.

The door opened, I recognised the Deads as the pregnant woman, she screamed in tremendous pain.

This is the first time I witnessed a Deads in any pain.

Another Deads stood at her side, male and made no attempt to come towards me. The woman let out one more scream, the bridge of the baby's head appeared, pushed from her cold dead vagina wall. One last ear piercing scream and the newborn landed on the blood covered floor with a thud together with the placenta. The terrified eyes of the earthling changed to an acceptance of what his destiny entailed. The baby lying lifeless on the floor reminded me of my miscarriage with our first attempt at having a child.

To my amazement the infant lifted himself up like a newborn deer, legs shaking as he tried to stand, the male Deads helped baby to its feet. Baby fell back to the ground and devoured the placenta. He stood again on his two legs and made a lunge at the earthling. The baby ravished at him like a hungry wolf on its first kill. Body flesh ripped apart, the crunching of bones made sure this young man had no hope of returning, all three Deads left no trace of the young mans existence.

They growled and snarled while pushing me to the side, I slid and fell to an empty floor. The new family ran from the cabin without hurting me, holding the baby in their arms.

The door opened, and fresh Irish air awakened me to the terror about to unfold here. In the moonlight I watched the last of the Deads disappear into the wood. The ship's clock struck midnight. The year now 2017, I had witnessed a miracle regarding Deads. For the first time on earth, a birth of a Deads occurred in an earthling's realm. The birth forced me to rethink my entire research. This child was not conceived from sex between two Deads, but from an earthling turned to a dead while carrying a baby. That Deads now became their protector. Soul mates for life.

Deads are now in Ireland, what have I done to my European allies? Delivering what can only be called, 'The Cruising Deads.'

Do not lose your earthanity towards Deads. May the Divine gods be with us all?

Disillusioned, I staggered towards Derry, in the distance a lady called for help. She was beautiful with long curly blond hair, a heart of gold and a colourful aurora radiating from her body. On her knees holding both her hands out towards me, a reminder of Desire.

[I called out in surprise, "Desire?" Time stopped. I was able to look around freely, no movements, the wind stood still, birds and leaves that where once flapping in the sky were stationary.

"Petre, Its Desire, I have missed you. "Donald Trump was voted the 45th president of the United States, by the remaining one million earthlings hiding in Alaska. As they rejoiced and cheered his claim of leading them back to freedom, the Deads claimed the final victory. Petre, I am dying, I am the LAST earthling, in the Western Hemisphere. My soul is departing my body and will rejoin the Realm of the Souls. Petre, don't despair on what you are about to discover..."]

My vision ended, and as I approached the distraught woman, I sensed a strong connection. I bent down and helped her up, a small bite mark on her neck became visible. Strange? The Deads hunger would be ravishing, why did they only bite her?

She pulled my head close and whispered:

"We have been waiting for you mother, do you not recognise me?" With her dying voice: "Please mother, protect your grandchildren they are hiding in the trees."

Tarmina, pointed towards an old oak tree, two beautiful children looking down and waving as they hung out of a tree house. I became speechless, overcome with joy and filled with complete sadness. A young and terrified Irish Man approached us with a long wooden spear shouting:

"Get out of the way, Get away, she has been bitten; I'm going to kill her!"

I shouted, "Leave my daughter alone!"

I placed myself in front to protect her, as I did, the spear pierced my chest and went straight through into Tarmina's sweet young heart. The tip protruded her back; we were both joined, close and connected. The last time we were this close was in my womb, now the spear represented the cord. Tarmina wrapped her arms around me, holding on tight with love, her final earthly hug. She slumped, falling backward, her hands fell away to the side towards the rough ground of this deadly planet.

The life faded from her body. My beautiful daughter had died and was taken from me yet again.

The blood drained from my body, dripping down the dirty spear and into Tarmina. The sky darkened, thunder and lightning followed with rain pouring from the heavens, tears from our Gods. In unbearable despair, I cried out, "How can this be, I am your chosen one."

No longer able to bear the weight of two, we tumbled to the wet ground. The spear kept us together; I lay on the Irish ground with vivid images of my life flashing before me. Earthlings are programmed to survive; my grandchildren gave me the strength to try, but the Divine gods had other plans.

With my final breath on earth, I said "...

The Story Continues in:
Volume 2 Derry Zombies, Bridge of Deads.

WIN PRIZES

by completing the crosswords.

In each crosswords, collect the characters in box 4 of each log. And submit the 24 letters to:
http://www.threezombiedogs.com/24letters

For your chance to win gift vouchers, T-Shirts, Mugs, books and lots more.

Check out our Online shop:

https://www.zazzle.com/thecruisingdeads

Log (-1)

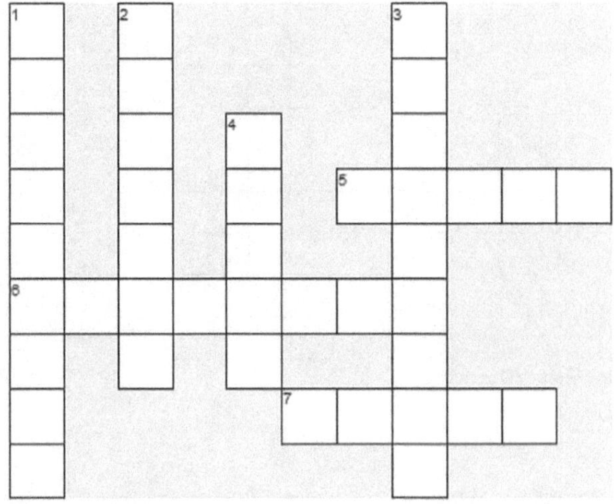

ThreeZombieDogs.com

ACROSS

5 Who was to sit on the world council
6 What occurred
7 1984 USA president

DOWN

1 Which country did they travel to
2 Which town did they travel to
3 Manx 1984 ? Coin
4 Number of remaining deads

Log (-0)

ThreeZombieDogs.com

ACROSS

3 What was special about the wolf
6 Name of heroes ship
7 How many hours away from the millennium

DOWN

1 Name of restaurant
2 Where are the chosen's ones children
4 What nationality is her friend
5 Chosen ones friend

Log 0

ACROSS

1 You will fear them
4 One of the fears of…
5 Name of fear
7 Color is the same

DOWN

2 DeadS want to eat them
3 The law should be
6 What is key to the realms

Log 1

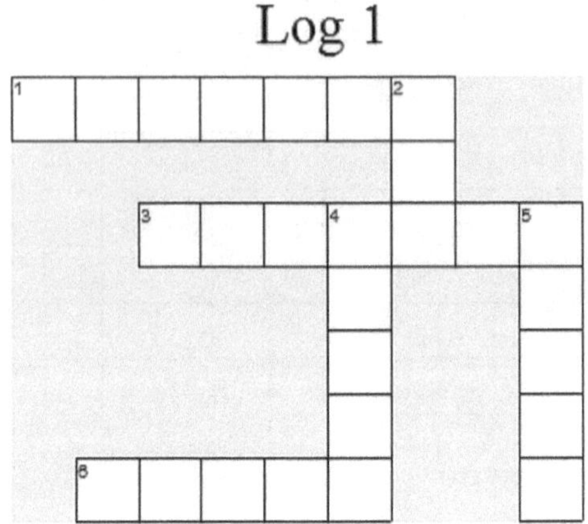

ACROSS

1 Where were the chosen ones first parents born
3 Dads best friend
6 What war killed 17 million

DOWN

2 Mothers name
4 What leg remained on his body
5 Where did the ship berth

Log 2

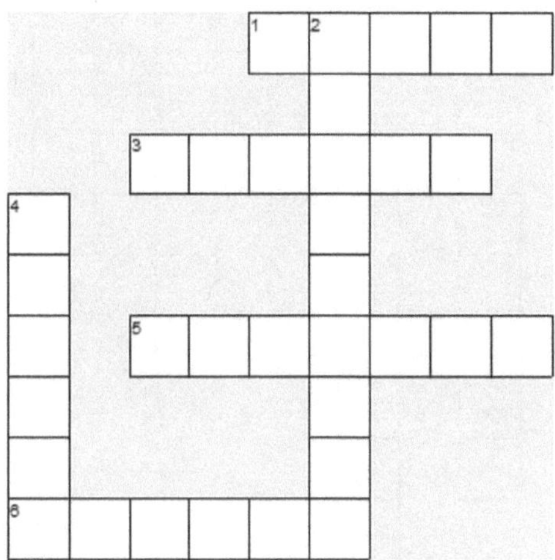

ACROSS

1 Who became President
3 University
5 Saved daughter
6 Country of lock down

DOWN

2 What type of DeadS do not leave bite-marks
4 What people need convinced to travel

Log 3

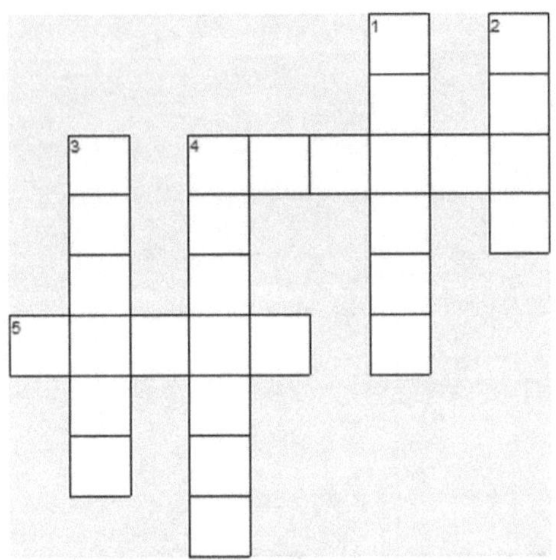

ACROSS

4 This is the new world of
5 What type of cotton was butchered into her mouth

DOWN

1 Her mouth was stitched
2 What type of blood, hit her face
3 They continue to be born
4 Who captured them

Log 4

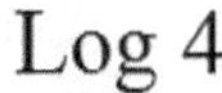

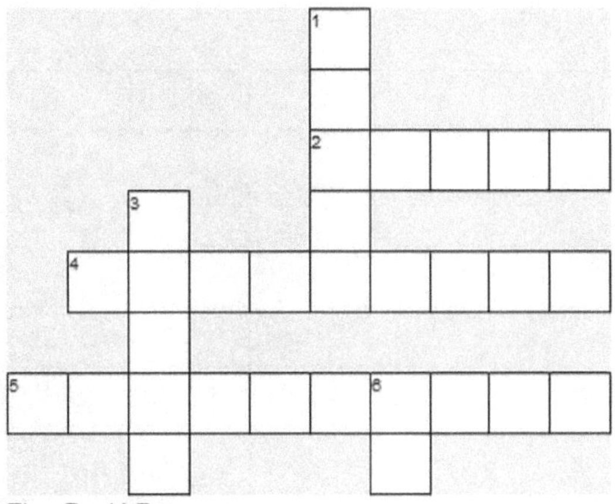

ThreeZombieDogs.com

ACROSS

2 Sensors were for a
4 Left on foot
5 They operated from their

DOWN

1 The type of aroma
3 My friend
6 Could you turn if blood from a DeadS splattered onto
   you

Log 5

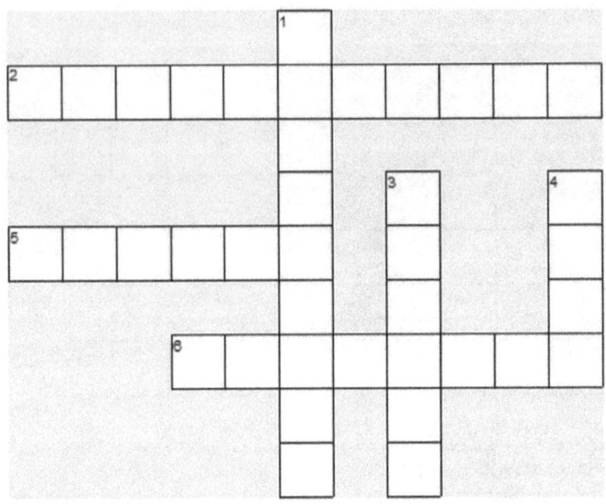

ACROSS

2 Another way of testing earthlings
5 Who first infected the American people
6 DeadS now feast on

DOWN

1 Only ferry allowed to travel from
3 Name of top scientist
4 Her base lasted how many years

Log 6

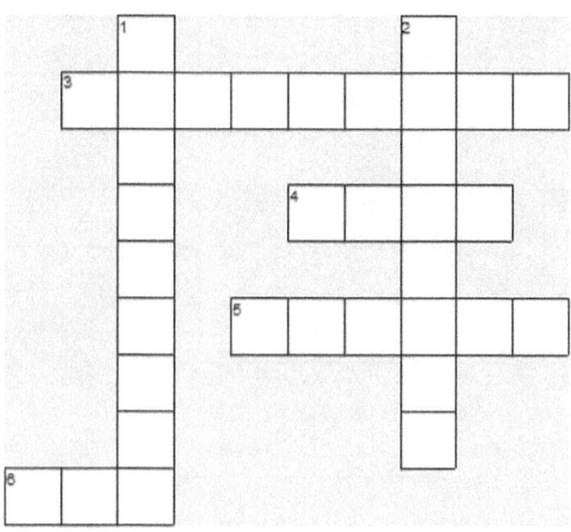

ACROSS

3 These evil earthlings were
4 Method of travel
5 Jazz Musician
6 The chosen on is not a

DOWN

1 The human meat was served
2 What's the name of the restaurant

Log 7

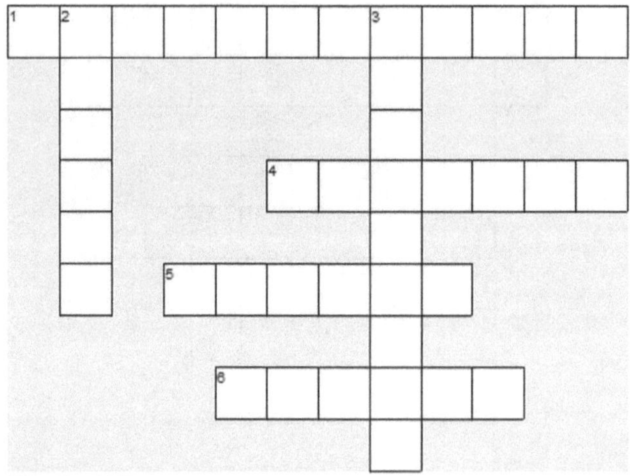

ThreeZombieDogs.com

ACROSS

1 …Parasitical bastards
4 I get my books from
5 It dripped onto the straw
6 A street car

DOWN

2 Desire dad was
3 Name of preservation

Log 8

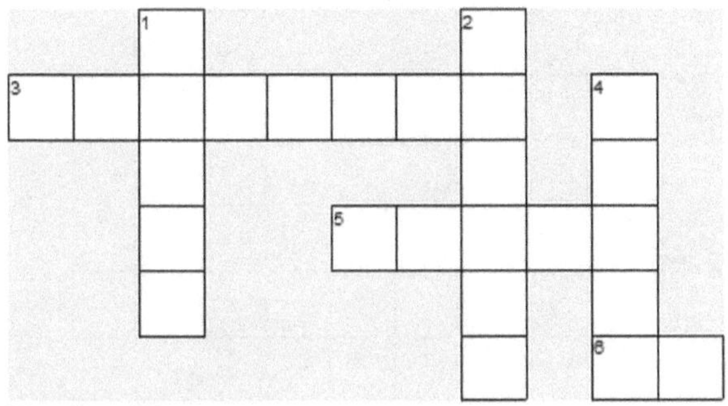

ACROSS

3 Clinics have all shut down
5 What was she asked to put down
6 babyWhat did the young girl scream

DOWN

1 Full of food
2 What type of attacks in 1775
4 What were one of the millions

Log 9

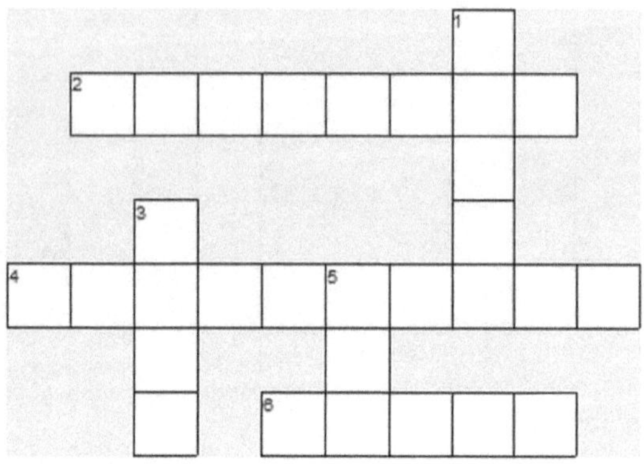

ACROSS

2 From side to side
4 His dance was a
6 In my state, another word for frisky

DOWN

1 She was only a child
3 Dragged from the room
5 How many walked from Folly Beach

Log 10

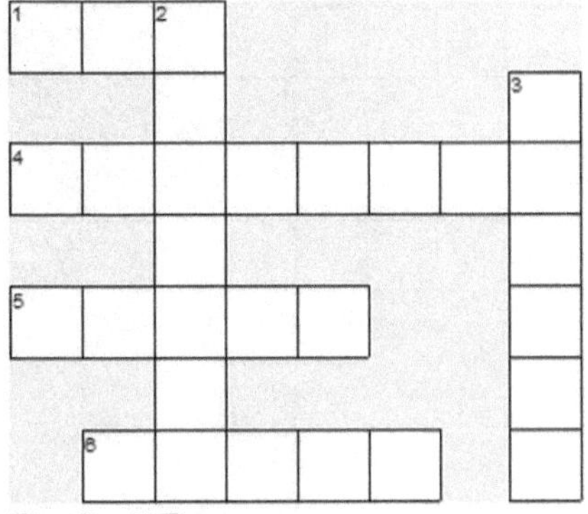

ACROSS

1 Jenna's grandad
4 Hybrid of vampire and vulture
5 The fish house
6 My name

DOWN

2 Jenna was a
3 The bridge

Log 11

ACROSS

1 She loved the ladies
4 The Town was called
5 Jo and
6 Type of Hotel

DOWN

2 Type of organ
3 HunterMy job

Log 12

ACROSS

2 Big dipper and
3 Fuel
5 We escaped on a
6 Who was she to meet

DOWN

1 Bad dream
4 The basket was full of

Log 13

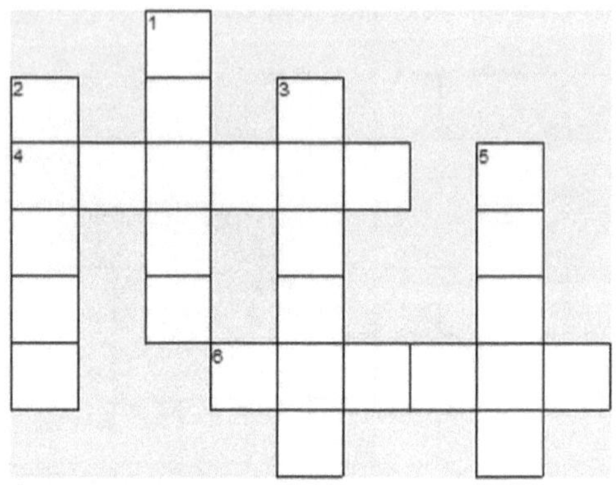

ACROSS

4 Remedy for vampires
6 Type of gods

DOWN

1 Hundred ships saved
2 Only country free from realms
3 Talked about vultures
5 When Chinese died they went to

Log 14

ACROSS

3 They can't live in
4 Do DeadS decay any further
5 Studied them for how many years
6 What country was doomed from internal fighting

DOWN

1 Europe brought the back
2 Drug of life

Log 15

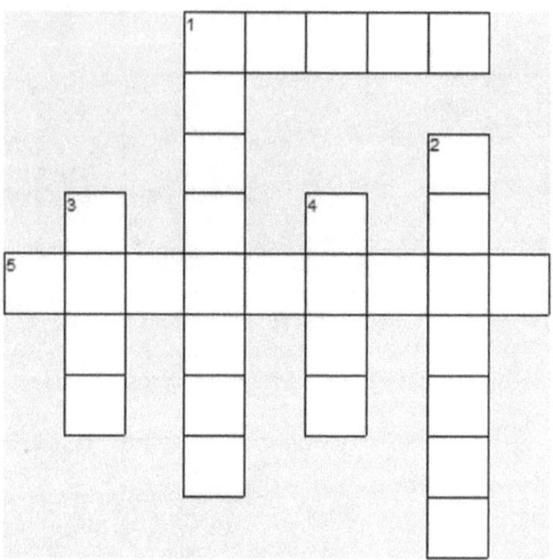

ACROSS

1 DeadS noise
5 I entered into a

DOWN

1 The factory made
2 The beginning of a
3 Fell into the river
4 It dragged her

Log 16

ACROSS

2 Fake name
5 Zombies were hidden by
6 Find out information by revisiting

DOWN

1 Type of deeds by evil's
3 They thought flesh eaters came from
4 One of the countries

Log 17

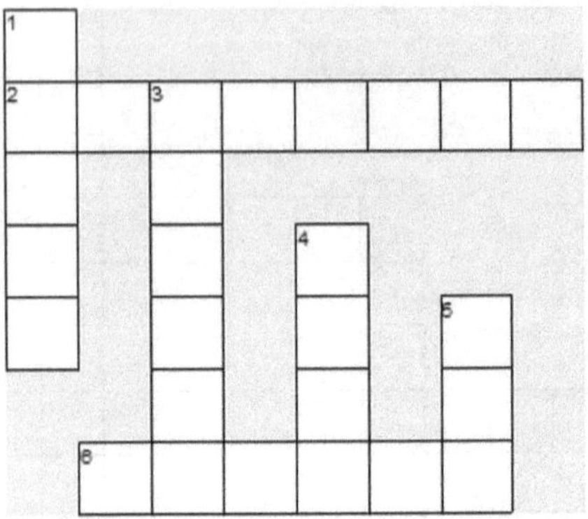

ACROSS

2 Earthlings are becoming
6 The chosen one felt like a

DOWN

1 The nurturing milk of life
3 The body becomes
4 Number of days at sea
5 Earthlings are refusing to

Log 18

ACROSS

2 What was happening to earthlings
4 hatred and prejudices against
5 The rituals
6 My Children are

DOWN

1 New Oreland rich in
3 Born and

Log 19

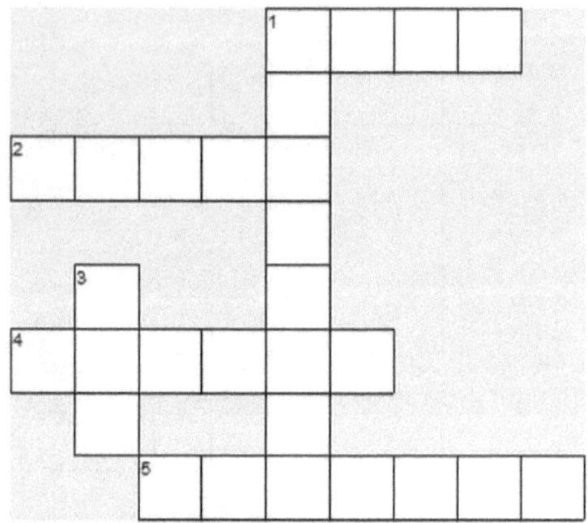

ACROSS

1 They were superstitious
2 Ship's captain
4 My colleague
5 His wife was a DeadS

DOWN

1 Disease spread by
3 It is spelt out

Log 20

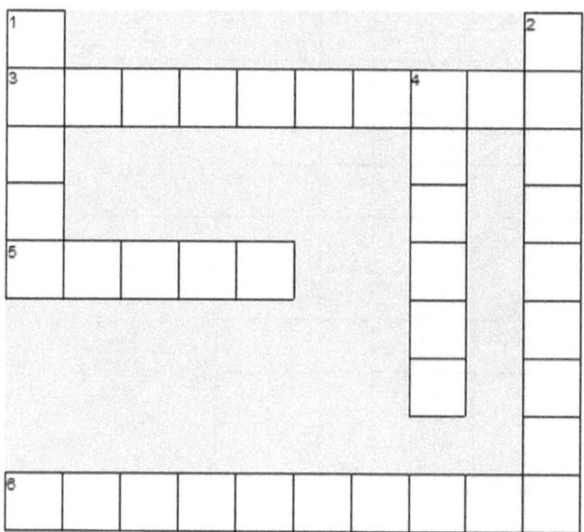

ACROSS

3 Traditions that will help find a cure
5 The Port of
6 Now a DeadS and pregnant

DOWN

1 She fed on a
2 A chosen one needs to come from my
4 It kept everyone away from the surgery

Log 21

ACROSS

2 My Daughter
3 Like a new born deer
4 What realm are the DeadS to rule
5 Reminded of

DOWN

1 The noise of earthling bones as they are chewed
4 Into her heart
5 We both

For Anyone Needing Help or if you can offer assistance.
Only some of the many organisations:

Samaritans & Child Line
http://www.samaritans.org/
https://www.childline.org.uk/

Suicide prevention
American Foundation: https://afsp.org/
UK Youth help https://www.papyrus-uk.org/
Ireland http://suicideprevention.ie/

Autism
UK: http://www.autism.org.uk/
USA: http://www.autism-society.org/
Ireland: http://autismireland.ie/

Cancer Support
https://www.standuptocancer.org.uk/
UK: http://www.cancerresearchuk.org/
http://www.macmillan.org.uk/
https://www.cancer.ie   https://cancerfocusni.org

Drug & Alcohol addiction
https://www.ncadd.org/about-addiction
http://addictionni.com/

These are only a few websites that can offer help.

If you can give help: Our Environment

Some of the many Organisations:

Greenpeace

http://www.greenpeace.org/international/en/

National Geographic

http://www.nationalgeographic.com/

Others

http://www.wildlifetrusts.org/

https://www.nationaltrust.org.uk/

http://www.wwf.org.uk/

http://www.sharktrust.org/

http://www.rainforestconservation.org/

The above list is not exhaustive by any means, take an interest and care about your environment. Do your research. All websites within this book, are subject to that websites rules and terms. We offer no validity for any websites. They are listed purely for reference.

Baseline Earthanity

Have you ever taken the time to watch regular Earthlings go about their daily duties? We take too much for granted in our fast paced existence. Even when we are watching sports, dancing, crafts, etc. It looks so easy, yet if you try, you soon realize it takes a lot of practice and skill. Well done to everyone that tries.

"You are not defined by the number of times you fall, but how many times you stand up!" Jo Malone.

Regardless of color, faith, creed, gender or country. And regardless of power, leadership, wealth or location on earth. NO ONE is superior to any other earthling. 'Every earthling on this planet is EQUAL,' that is baseline common sense. AND earthanity as it was meant to be. Every earthling deserves the right to live in peace and harmony. Abusing that is 'inequality.'

Since my birth in Bonnie Scotland, storytelling was a fabric of my upbringing, I loved hearing stories and enjoyed telling them. Now it's time to put pen to paper. I would like to thank my Aunt Jean, mum and dad, all now in the realm of the souls for the endless stories they would tell us. I'm releasing a series of children's stories in their memory. My brother Jim for supporting me in all my endeavors and Rik and Jean for putting up with my antics, including making vases out of their LP collection and much more.

I want my books to have a hint of reality mixed in with all that fiction. To stop one in their tracks to think. Did that happen? Could that happen? Is that person real? What can I do to make this earth a better place? I want the reader to be engaged, have fun and to immerse themselves into the story, to be there in the front line. I want the reader to utilize their imagination and construct their personal imagery within my stories.

Derry, the city of Culture is now our home. Few years ago, I went back to University as a mature student and completed a three-year degree. Who ever said students had it easy? I had forgotten what it was like to be a student, give me work any-day!

During my winter break my eldest son and I went for a trip to Amsterdam. The snow was slushy on the ground and we left the hotel to walk to a nearby cafe for some breakfast. My laces weren't tied, so my boots slipped backward and forwards. Instead of walking normal as everyone else does, I dragged and slid my boots through the snow, without lifting my legs in an attempt to keep the boots attached to my feet. My son looked at me and said: "Would you stop that, you're acting like a student and showing me up." I replied: "I'am a student!"

We are all students of life, and sometimes we get bogged down with what is termed 'normal,' and forget the real mystery of life itself.

You can get in touch by sending a message to any address below. If you would like a visit to your book club or bookstore, drop me a note.

Many thanks for taking the time to read my book.

Divad Thims.

https://www.threezombiedogs.com/

https://www.zazzle.com/thecruisingdeads

You

Are not

Alone in the universe